HER WICKED **HERO**
A BLACK DAWN NOVEL
BOOK 4

CAITLYN O'LEARY

© Copyright 2018 Caitlyn O'Leary
All rights reserved.
All cover art and logo © Copyright 2018
By Passionately Kind Publishing Inc.
Cover by Lori Jackson Design
Editing by Sandy Ebel - Personal Touch Editing

All rights reserved. No part of this book may be reproduced in any form or by any electronic or mechanical means, including information storage and retrieval systems—except in the case of brief quotations embodied in critical articles or reviews—without permission in writing from the author.

This book is a work of fiction. The names, characters, and places portrayed in this book are entirely products of the author's imagination or used fictitiously. Any resemblance to actual events, locales, or persons, living or dead, is entirely coincidental and not intended by the author.

The unauthorized reproduction or distribution of this copyrighted work is illegal. Criminal copyright infringement, including infringement without monetary gain, is investigated by the FBI and is punishable by up to five years in federal prison and a fine of $250,000.

If you find any eBooks being sold or shared illegally, please contact the author at Caitlyn@CaitlynOLeary.com.

DEDICATION

Dedicated to those who are serving and who have served.

SYNOPSIS

She Needs a Hero

Marcia Price knows she's in the hands of a monster. Kidnapped at gunpoint and dragged deeper and deeper into the Borneo's jungle, she wants to give up. But dammit, no matter what, she *will* survive this, even if it almost kills her. And maybe, just maybe, the universe will send her a hero.

He'll Move Heaven and Earth

A photograph. A feeling. A knowing. That's all it takes for Dante "Zed" Zaragoza to realize his fate is intertwined with a woman he's never met, a woman in the clutches of a sociopath. Zed will need more than his usual bag of tricks if he's going to find Marcia Price and bring her home safely. That photograph means she's alive...for now. Lucky for Marcia, Zed's a trained Navy SEAL.

Unfortunately, so is the man who has Marcia...

CHAPTER ONE

"He's going into anaphylactic shock, I need the EpiPen," she screamed.

Christie and Debbie were crying as Harold Brockman was having seizures in the dirt.

"If he dies, there's no need for the rest of you, so you better find it fast," Raymond said as he emptied out the contents of a duffle bag onto the floor of the hut. Out of the corner of her eye, she saw him light a cigar and watch her search.

Marcia tried to block out the two young girls' sobs. She hated the subterfuge, but their lives depended on it. She saw the small black case with the EpiPens, but she couldn't find the freaking pocket watch. She scrabbled through the mess of accumulated crap until she spied something round and gold.

"Hurry up, girlie, your reason for living is dying."

She had just seconds. Marcia fumbled for the clasp and popped open the watch, then depressed the glass. She felt it click, then she jammed it shut. It couldn't have been that easy, could it? God, she hoped so. She dropped the watch and grabbed the little black case.

"Found it," she shouted in triumph as she held up the container that held the medicine. Now she had to pretend that she was administering the drug without doing it. So far, Mr. B. was a darn fine actor, hopefully, she would be as good. She crouched down beside her best friend's father and took out the syringe. It looked straightforward. She pulled off the blue cap, then held it with her hand near the orange top and jammed it into his thigh, making sure the needle didn't enter his flesh.

After a few seconds, Harold Brockman took a deep gasping breath. Boy, he was good. They must have taught that in spy school. Marcia started to shake. She looked up at Raymond. He was staring at her with those dead eyes. She hated him. She hated all of them, but Raymond was the worst. He had smiled when he killed the three mathematicians. He'd enjoyed it. He'd used a knife on one of them. Hadn't even shot him.

"Pick that shit up," Raymond said. He motioned to everything on the ground with his cigar. When Marcia crawled over to the bag, Christie and Debbie practically fell into their father's arms. Even though he had broken ribs, he didn't flinch, instead, assuring them he was okay.

"So, you live for another day," Raymond laughed. Marcia flinched when the ashes he flicked hit her cheek.

"The girls need more food and water."

"What about you? Aren't you going to ask for yourself? Or is big sister too much of a martyr?"

Marcia went along with that lie as well. Harold Brockman had told his two girls she needed to pretend to be his eldest daughter, Lesley Brockman, she would be safer that way. Marcia appreciated Mr. B. looking out for her, but she also knew it might eventually wind up taking some of the focus off the younger girls, so she went along with the ploy.

"Yes, Dad and I need more food and water too, but it's more important for the girls."

Raymond flicked his cigar at her again and if she hadn't dodged it, ash would have gone into her eye. He cracked a smile, this time, it reached his eyes. "What are you willing to do for the extras, Lesley?"

"Nothing," Harold choked out. "Don't play your stupid games with her. You need your hostages in good working order, so get us food and water. God knows, it's plentiful around here," the older man said disdainfully.

"You're not in a good position to give orders, Brockman."

Marcia knelt there, looking back and forth between a man she considered her surrogate father to the scariest man she had ever encountered in her life.

"Sure I am. I'm the biggest fish you've ever had on a hook. What are the bids up to? Twenty million?" Harold Brockman asked.

"Higher. Especially with the leverage we can provide. You'll sing like a canary. Every American secret will become available to whoever buys you."

"They ought to know better, they've changed everything since I've retired from the NSA. God knows, once they figure out I've been kidnapped, they'll re-evaluate every policy too."

"You're dead, didn't you know that? You died with everybody else on that yacht. Hell, it was my vote to leave two of your other kids on that fucking boat too, so I had less to worry about. But Kyle thought you'd bring more if we sold you with three daughters who could be tortured to get you to talk."

Marcia rolled up onto her feet and pushed her face into Raymond's. "Enough," she ground out. "Don't talk that way in front of my sisters."

"She's right," Kyle said as he bent to come into the hut. "What the fuck are you thinking? We need to keep these young girls calm."

Kyle cupped Marcia's cheek. "You okay?"

She forced herself not to flinch away from his touch. He was the leader of the mercenaries, and she couldn't afford to alienate him.

"I'm fine."

"Raymond, go check on the professor and her husband. We want to make sure all of our assets are taken care of." Marcia watched as the monster picked up his backpack and ducked out the door.

"How is Ilsa?" Marcia asked. She remembered how one of the men had used the butt of his rifle on her. She had doubled over onto the ground.

"Lesley, you really need to keep your focus on your family," Kyle admonished.

She swallowed. She didn't know why she had thought he was nicer. All of these men scared her to death, but she knew she couldn't let it show. That was one of the things she had learned from Mr. B. She swallowed and said confidently, "We need more food and water,"

"Done. Was that so hard to ask for?" His pleasant voice made her skin crawl.

"How much longer are we going to be here?" Christie asked.

"Probably no more than a week, then you'll have someplace lovely to stay," Kyle smiled.

Harold was propped up against the wall of the hut, holding his twelve and thirteen-year-old daughters in his arms, his face ashen with pain.

Kyle left the small hut, and Marcia listened for the padlock to click into place. She crawled over to Harold, and he held out his hand for her and she took it.

"Did you get it done?" he asked.

"Yes."

"Then help is on its way."

* * *

"You coming?" Hunter Diaz asked.

"Just want to study this a bit longer. I won't be late," Zed assured him.

Hunter considered him before finally nodding and leaving the small briefing room. Dante 'Zed' Zaragoza sat back down in the seat that Lieutenant Gray Taylor had vacated and opened the file of the ten passengers and six crew members who had supposedly died. But Zed *knew* some of them were still alive. At least for now.

He looked around the gray room inside the USS Ronald Reagan, a nuclear-powered supercarrier. He was surrounded by the most advanced technology in the world and currently assisting one of the deadliest SEAL teams on the planet, and here he was knocked on his ass by the strongest feeling of his life. Not something normal people felt, but a gut-deep intuition, a *knowing*. Thirty-six years on this planet and not once had his instincts steered him wrong.

He leafed through the file again. Heavy hitters from around the world had been on this yacht. They had just lectured in Singapore and their next stop was Hong Kong. The poor bastards had thought it would be a cool mini-vacation for their families. Instead of five days in the lap of luxury, the world now thought they'd been blown to bits in the South China Sea.

Zed pulled out the two photos and a short write-up on the Brockman family. Harold Brockman was the key to this mess, he just knew it. Brockman was the former head of the NSA who had retired to write books. Zed liked his books, but a lot of people didn't. He looked at the photo of his family that was two years old, his wife and three daughters. It had been taken a month before his wife had died of a brain embolism. In it, the girls were ten, eleven, and twenty-two.

Only the two youngest girls had gone on the trip, the oldest was in rehab. That was the reason for the second photo. Marcia Price, a girl who somewhat resembled the Brockman daughters, at least with her brown curly hair and dark eyes, but that was where the similarities ended. This girl's spirit radiated off the photo. According to the intel, she had come along to keep the younger girls entertained while the father lectured and wrote.

Zed knew down to his toes Marcia was alive. So were some of the others, but absolutely, positively, Marcia was alive. Even more, he knew his fate was destined to be intertwined with this woman. The only other feeling that had been this strong and personal revolved around one of his best friends, Hunter Diaz.

Searches were being done all along their last known coordinates. Every nation involved, including China, had been called in to search for the dignitaries' missing yacht. It was assumed it had capsized, but what few people knew was there had been a boat shadowing the yacht at all times. The South China Sea was known for pirates, and there wasn't a chance in hell Brockman was going to be gallivanting off without proper precautions. As soon as the yacht hit international waters, the other boat, known as a floating armory started shadowing them. The armory was loaded for bear when it came to men and weapons. The men were some damned fine former

American, British, and Australian military personnel, and their job was to follow the yacht all the way to Hong Kong.

The fact the armory went silent the same time the yacht had, raised all kinds of alarms in the U.S. This wasn't some kind of boating accident, this was something else entirely.

Zed traced the line of Marcia's jaw on her photo, then forced himself to stop. He arranged the file back together, headed out the door, and down the narrow hall.

"We've got something," Gray said as he stuck his head out of the locker room. "Get a move on."

Zed felt his lip curl upwards. It was about fucking time.

* * *

The Reagan had been positioned four-hundred miles from Borneo where the signal had originated. They had done aerial recon, but with no luck. The jungle was too dense, they were in the middle of the Pinangah Forest Reserve. Further investigation found the armory boat docked close to the Northern most tip of the island, near the nation of Brunei. Two men were spotted topside. Intel was imperative to determine what they would find in the jungle. It was decided to capture the men at the boat and question them.

The team landed in a small airfield an hour away from the harbor where the boat was docked. Transport was waiting for them in the form of two SUVs. It was a tight fit for the eight big men. Dex Evans, their communications and tech guru, had his computer open on this lap.

"Anything?" Zed asked.

"The beacon hasn't moved from yesterday," Dex told him, pointing to the same spot on the map. The yacht had gone missing ten days ago. The trek from the harbor to that spot in the middle of Borneo would have taken five days with the novices.

"One new thing," Gray said as they sped down the highway to the harbor.

Zed raised an eyebrow.

"A Chinese cargo ship spotted the remains of the yacht. They've got everyone converging on the site to determine what happened and search for survivors."

"Sure would be nice," Wyatt said.

Nobody responded.

"I want to go over that again," Dex said raising his head. "There are some things that are definitely off when I go over the records of the men who were supposedly on the armory."

"What do you mean?" Gray asked.

"Lieutenant, I already sent this stuff to Langley. It started with the Australian, Seymore Gates. When I dug into his record, everything looked perfect. That is until I cross-referenced it to his social media presence, then I found out he's currently on his honeymoon."

"Shit," Griffin Porter said. "If one of these guys is sideways, they all could be."

"Exactly," Dex said grimly. "I just caught this ten minutes ago. I'm pissed I wasn't checking them on social media back on the aircraft carrier, that was pure fucking stupidity on my part."

"Are you out of your mind?" Gray said. "Shit, Dex, Langley and the NSA are going to fire some of their people over this. They were in charge of vetting the people tasked to protect the former head of the National Security Agency. Chances are, you're going to get recruited… again!"

"No more boots for you, Dex," Dalton laughed, "nothing but spit-shined shoes. You'll love it in Virginia."

Gray turned to his team members and glared. "You're all stuck on this team until I personally kick you the hell off, are we clear?"

"Aye aye, Lieutenant," Aiden O'Malley said, smothering a grin. Zed liked Gray's second in command. He was a take no prisoners type of guy.

Gray slowly turned to look at Zed, his eyes narrowed. "That includes you Zaragoza for the time being. You're stuck too." He focused his attention back on Dex. "How many more of these guys do you think are bogus?" Gray asked as he waved to Dex's computer.

"Hold on." Dex's fingers were flying over the keyboard. "I'm checking on the commander of the boat."

Zed peered over his shoulder and saw screen after screen pop up. He didn't know how Dex could possibly be comprehending any of the information being shown.

"Come on, come on baby, come to Papa," Dex muttered.

Suddenly an American Express statement came up, and Dex kept it up on screen for almost thirty seconds, then he popped over to the Kentucky DMV and found a picture that matched the name on the Amex bill. After that, he pulled up one from Walter Lowell's Army file with him wearing his green beret. He was retired Special Forces, and according to his American Express bill, he'd just been to Disneyland two days ago.

Dex turned to look at Gray and the rest of the team. "If he's a fraud and the Aussie was a fraud, my guess is every last one of them was."

"Then who are we dealing with?" Wyatt asked.

"Mercenaries. Some very smart and competent mercs. Did you see where any fingerprints or photos were taken of these clowns when they were hired?" Griff asked.

"What do you think?" Dex gave a look of disgust.

"Hey, a guy can hope," Griff said.

"So, we're dealing with eleven, soon to be nine mercenaries who we can't identify," Griff said.

Zed, Hunter, and Aiden shared a look.

Gray caught it and grimaced, but Zed noted he didn't shut them down. They needed to know what they were up against, and one of those two men on the boat were going to provide that information, come hell or high water.

CHAPTER TWO

"You need to sleep," Harold said in a barely there whisper. He eased himself down beside her, so they were sitting against the wall of the hut, staring at the locked door.

Marcia looked at the man she had come to love almost as much as she had her own dad. "I just can't, Mr. B."

"Lesley, you need to call me Dad at all times."

It was freaky hearing him call her Lesley. It was almost like it was bad luck or something, that they were wishing Lesley harm.

"You're thinking too hard about this. Would it be easier if I just called you Honey?"

Marcia nodded. "Do you really think someone's going to find us?"

"Definitely. Now can you sleep?"

Marcia shook her head, then scowled as she felt her dirty hair hit her face. "Ever since they drugged us, so they could take us off the boat to wherever we are, I just can't seem to close my eyes. I'm too scared I'll wake up somewhere even worse."

"Honey, the girls need you. They need you fully functioning, and instead, you've been fading. What you accomplished with the EpiPen was fantastic. You got us help."

She stared up at Harold Brockman, looking for reassurance. "What if I did it wrong?"

"You didn't. I've known you damn near your whole life, you did it perfectly. We just need to be ready when help arrives."

"What happens if Raymond goes somewhere with the backpack? I should never have put it back there." Marcia hit her fist on her thigh. "That was so stupid."

"It isn't his, it's a duffel they put everything in, it's not going anywhere. Haven't you noticed, all the men are still wearing their regular packs?"

She wanted to believe him, she really did. But she would have felt better if it was with them.

"I have to depend on you to follow orders," his voice turned to steel. "If they had found that watch on you, they would have beat you or worse. Then they would have destroyed the beacon and moved all of us. Our lives depend on you doing what I tell you." He put his knuckles under her chin. "Look at me."

She raised her eyes.

He started coughing, but she watched him will himself to stop. She was so worried about his injuries. "Now my family doesn't know this. My wife didn't even know this, but I've been in a situation similar to this in the past. I know what I'm doing. I know what needs to be done to survive. You have to do what I tell you. If you don't, we'll die."

"You really were a spy, weren't you?"

"If I tell you, then I'll have to kill you," he said with a wan grin.

She smiled, trying to perk him up. "Did you have a number? Were you 008?"

"That's for the British. We came up with code names like Rambo. Seriously though, I need you alert for whatever comes next. I'm depending on you. That means you need to get some shut-eye. I'm on watch, you sleep. Then when you wake up, we can switch. How does that sound?" He coughed again.

It actually sounded good. Marcia pulled the thin blanket tighter around herself. She stretched out and placed her arms under her head and looked over at Debbie and Christie. Knowing she needed to be rested for them had her closing her eyes.

Marcia felt rather than heard when Debbie stood over her. "What is it Sweets?" she asked the girl.

"I need to go," she said nodding toward the door.

There was a makeshift outhouse their captors had made near the edge of the clearing. It offered a bit of privacy, and Marcia always went with the girls. She looked at Harold and saw he was awake but sweating a lot. He gave a tight grin and nod. Those ribs of his had to be hurting pretty bad. She'd insist he take off his shirt and then bind him with a torn blanket when she returned.

"Okay, Debbie, let's go." She banged on the door. "Bathroom break," she shouted.

Of course, there was no answer. Even though it was the afternoon and she could hear noise outside, they always took their damn time to let them out. She gave it two minutes, then banged on the door even louder.

"Bathroom break," she yelled again. She turned to Christie who was still on the floor, clutching her blanket around her. She knew she hated going to the latrine and held off for as long as she could, but she needed to take advantage.

"Christie, come with us."

The younger girl shook her head.

"Christie, go with the other girls," Harold said.

"No. I want to stay with you. I don't have to go. I promise."

Marcia looked at the water bottle next to Christie and realized it was almost full. Mr. Brockman must have seen it too.

"Christie, you have to drink your water, otherwise, you'll get sick. Drink some right now."

"No." Christie didn't look twelve, she looked five years old sitting in the middle of the dirt floor of the hut as she stared petulantly at her father.

"Young lady, I said drink it."

"Fine." Christie picked up the bottle and started drinking, and Debbie banged on the door of the hut. It opened.

"Keep your pants on," Raymond laughed. "Oh yeah, you're not, are you? Follow me, I'm your guide."

Debbie grabbed Marcia's hand in a death grip as they walked across the little clearing toward the lean-to that housed the communal toilet which was nothing more than wooden planks over a hole in the ground.

"Wait here." Marcia looked inside before she would let Debbie go. She wanted to make sure there were no snakes or spiders. Marcia came back out. "Where's the toilet paper?" she demanded.

"We're out," Raymond smirked.

"Kyle said he made sure there would be some for the girls."

"He was wrong."

Marcia grabbed Debbie's hand. "I'm going to find him." She started walking away with the girl in tow. Raymond grabbed her upper arm and whirled her around.

"Bitch. You'll do what I say. We're out of goddamn toilet paper. The little girl can go find a fucking leaf."

"No!" a woman shrieked

Raymond, Marcia, and Debbie all whirled around to stare when they saw Mr. Hoff being dragged out of his hut with his sobbing wife following him.

"Raymond, get over here," Kyle called.

"Come on, let's join the party." Raymond grabbed both of their arms and fast-walked them over to where the Hoff's were.

"I have good news," Kyle said grinning to the nine mercenaries standing around the Hoff's. "We just made our first sale."

Another man Marcia hated, his name was Kroeger, he pulled out his knife and started cleaning his nails. "So now that there's less for us to watch, you going to start paying us off and letting us go on our merry way?" he asked Kyle.

"Is that what you want to do? Do you want to be released early from the job?" Kyle asked.

"I'm sick of the jungle. You're getting paid now. It could be weeks before the other deals are made. So yeah, I want out early."

"Okay, that can be arranged." Kyle nodded to the bald man who was next to Kroeger, and somehow, he'd shot Kroeger in the head before Marcia even saw him pull out his gun.

Mrs. Hoff started to scream hysterically. Debbie started to cry. Marcia pulled her into her arms, shoving the young girl's face into her chest, so she couldn't look at the bloody mess.

"Nice going, Kyle, more for us. How much is Hoff going for?" Raymond asked.

"He's small potatoes compared to the physicist and Brockman, he only went for six million."

"Cool, he's the six-million-dollar man," the bald man said.

"You girls are going to be with us a while," Raymond whispered to Marcia and Debbie. "Your daddy's worth a fortune."

Debbie whimpered, but Marcia had had enough. "If he's so important, where the heck is our fricking toilet paper?" she said loud enough for Kyle to hear.

"Bitch," Raymond said under his breath.

"You've got balls, Lesley," Kyle chuckled. "I like that. Raymond, give them a roll of toilet paper to keep. They'll have to make it last."

Raymond let go of her arm and stomped off. Marcia breathed a sigh of relief. She knew it was going to be badly bruised. She watched as Raymond tried to go past Kyle, but the man shoved Raymond in the chest and whispered in his ear. Raymond paled, then he turned to glare at Marcia. Kyle pushed him away toward the mercenaries' quarters.

"Come on, Franz, let's get you and Lilith going. You've got a boat to catch. Need to start your trek through the jungle. Then you get to take a nice nap again. You remember that, don't you?" Kyle asked.

Mrs. Hoff started talking in German to her husband. Kyle backhanded her. "English. Speak in English."

She hit the ground hard and didn't get up. It took a moment for Marcia to realize her head had hit a rock.

"Fuck me," Kyle said disgustedly. He yanked her up by her arm and shook her. "Lilith, are you with me?" She moaned.

"Well, at least you're not dead. Now, speak English."

She looked up at him helplessly. "Where are we going?"

"There are some nice people in Tehran who want to talk to your husband about his banking practices."

"Can't you let her go? I'll tell them anything they want to know. Can't she be set free?" Mr. Hoff begged.

"Franz, you're a big boy. You know everyone likes to have a bit of influence when negotiating with someone. She's their way of influencing you."

Marcia watched as Mr. Hoff started to cry. Then like magic, Mrs. Hoff stopped. "It's going to be okay Franz. I'll be fine. We'll both be fine. You'll see."

Raymond stomped back and shoved the roll into Marcia's chest. "I'm going to get you for this." He grabbed her and pulled so hard, she hit her knees. "Get up."

Debbie looked at Marcia, her fright obvious. Marcia gave her the best smile she could and got off the ground. Raymond damn near sprinted to the lean-to, and the girls did their best to keep up. Marcia handed the roll of toilet paper to Debbie and stood in front of the opening to give her privacy from Raymond. She also didn't want Debbie to be able to see anything happening with the Hoff's.

"Bull, you're going to go with Kevin, I want you back tomorrow. Duane isn't answering at the boat. He's probably drinking again. If he is, you know what to do," Kyle said.

Marcia saw the man named Bull nod his head. What the heck that meant, she had no idea. At least, he seemed kind the way he helped Mrs. Hoff to her feet. God, what was going to happen to them when they got to Tehran? Were they really going to torture Mrs. Hoff? Surely Mr. Hoff would just tell them everything he knew. She knew Mr. Brockman would because he wouldn't want anything to happen to Christie or Debbie.

What happened if they didn't believe him? What happened if they thought he wasn't telling them everything? She covered her mouth, sure she was going to throw up.

"Marcia, are you all right?" Debbie asked as she came out of the outhouse.

"Who's Marcia?" Raymond demanded.

"That's my middle name," Marcia quickly lied. "Lesley Marcia Brockman."

Raymond stared at her for a moment, then looked back at the spectacle in the clearing where the Hoff's were being led away. Mrs. Hoff was trying to comfort her husband.

"Look at how weak he is," Raymond said. "You can totally see he doesn't wear the pants in that family," he laughed. "Same damn thing with the professor and her husband. Damn, all these pussy-whipped men, it's pathetic."

Debbie handed the roll of toilet paper to Marcia. "It's your turn. I'll stand guard."

Raymond laughed again. "What are you going to guard against, little girly?"

"Debbie, just stay close, okay?" Marcia said quietly. She waited until the girl nodded, then went into the lean-to. Marcia finished quickly and was zipping up her jeans when three loud blasts sounded right outside.

"Debbie," she screamed, sure the girl had been shot even though she could see she had just ducked down. Marcia lunged out of the opening and tackled her to the ground, covering her with her body.

"Fuck," Raymond yelled. Marcia looked up and saw he had pulled his huge pistol out of its holster and had it aimed into the clearing. She looked over to see what he was aiming at. The two men who had been holding the Hoff's were now lying in a pool of blood. Mrs. Hoff was screaming again. She saw two of Kyle's men behind the hut where Christie and Harold were, and they were shooting into the jungle. Where was Kyle? Were they about to be rescued?

More shots were fired. Another one of the mercenaries ran over to the Hoff's and grabbed Mr. Hoff, putting a gun to his head.

"Stop shooting, or I'll kill him," he shouted to the unknown assailants in the jungle.

The shooting stopped, and Marcia breathed a sigh of relief. At least there wouldn't be any more holes shot into the hut with Mr. B. and Christie. Then she saw blood spray at the same time as she heard the crack of a rifle. The head of the man holding Mr. Hoff just disintegrated. Marcia stared in disbelief as Mr. Hoff and the dead man both fell to the ground.

"Franz," Mrs. Hoff screamed at the top of her lungs. She crawled over to her husband. She screamed again as her leg spurted blood. Oh God, she'd been shot. Marcia tried to cover Debbie even more, not wanting the precious girl to be hurt.

So many shots rang out through the clearing, Marcia felt dizzy. She tried to see what was going on, wanting to know if they were going to live or not. She prayed all the bad guys would die, and they would be rescued.

She shrieked as her hair was wrenched almost out of her head. She was on her knees. She desperately tried to pull out of Raymond's grasp, so she could protect Debbie.

"Stop it. You're coming with me."

"Marcia," the young girl wailed.

Raymond pointed the gun at the Debbie. Shots continued to ring out. Then, like avenging angels, Marcia saw men painted in green and wearing green fatigues running into the clearing. They shot Kyle.

Her hair was yanked so hard, she was lifted onto her feet. "I will kill your sister." Raymond's eyes looked crazy. Marcia looked down and saw his gun was pointed at Debbie's head.

"Don't go," Debbie begged.

"What do you want?" Marcia asked.

"You're my insurance policy. I'll get a payoff as long as I have you. Now, let's go."

When Marcia hesitated, he hit Debbie in the head with the muzzle of the rifle. She let out a cry and slumped to the ground. He lifted the rifle butt again and stared at Marcia.

"It's your choice."

"Stop! I'll go with you."

He fisted his hand in her curls and yanked. She did her best to keep up with him, trying not to cry despite the pain. It wasn't until they were well past the clearing and lost in the jungle, she realized her jeans weren't even buttoned.

* * *

"Count off," Gray commanded. "I want to know how many bogeys you got."

"One," Dalton said.

"Two," Hunter said.

"One," Aiden said.

"One," Dex said.

"Two," Zed said as he prowled into the clearing. He counted three prisoner huts and one larger dwelling for the mercs. Aiden was kneeling down next to an old man and woman, his backpack already off, so he could offer first-aid.

"I'm counting eight bodies, Lieutenant," Griff said to Gray Tyler. "Either someone's being bashful, or there was a falling out amongst these assholes, and they killed one of their own."

Zed watched as Aiden talked to the older couple, then spoke up. "The leader executed one of the men before we got here according to Mrs. Hoff." That still left them down one mercenary. According to Duane on the boat, there were nine guys up here at the camp, and Zed was positive he hadn't been lying. He'd been in too much pain to lie.

"I've got Brockman, and he's in bad shape," Dex called from one of the huts.

"I've got two injured," Griff yelled, from another hut.

Zed scanned the area carefully, he felt something. That's when he heard it. A whimper over at the edge of the clearing.

"Nobody in the barracks," Dalton said disgustedly. He and Wyatt came out and went to Aiden. He saw Dalton get some of Aiden's supplies and head into the hut with Dex as Zed started jogging toward the soft sound of a girl crying. He saw the makeshift latrine, and the closer he got to it, he could smell the stench.

"Hello?" he queried. "Who are you? It's safe to come out."

There was no answer. He crouched down, knowing his size was formidable. Even though he was pretty sure that he was dealing with an innocent, he kept his rifle at the ready since there was still one mercenary unaccounted for. A girl who couldn't be more than thirteen peeked around the corner, her brown hair was matted with blood.

"He took her," she gasped. "You have to save her."

Zed moved toward her, "*Querida*, I have to look at your head."

She shook her head, then moaned. "What?"

"Honey, you're hurt."

Enough of this happy horseshit. Zed pushed his rifle behind his back and had the girl up in his arms before she could blink.

"Please, help Marcia," she said again in a whisper. "He's got her."

"I will," he promised. "You need to be quiet, so we can help you, right now." He eased her down on the ground next to the older couple he recognized as the Hoff's. "Where are the others?" he asked Aiden quietly.

"My sister and dad are in there," the girl struggled to sit up as she pointed at one of the huts.

"What's your name?" Aiden asked as he crouched down beside her. He already had a sterile pad against her head and was flashing a penlight in her eyes. "Look forward for me, will you?" he smiled easily at the girl.

"You're not listening to me." She grabbed at Zed's arm, ignoring Aiden. "I'm fine. You need to go after Marcia. That man will kill her." Her eyes flooded with tears.

The kid was killing *him*. He loved her concern for Marcia. Every instinct inside him was screaming to do exactly what she wanted. He needed to go after Marcia and bring her back to safety.

"Gray, we've got a problem," Zed heard Hunter shout out to the lieutenant. "Come here."

"I'll be right back, I promise." Zed squeezed the girl's hand and went over to see what Hunter had found. He was examining one of the corpses and had rolled up the man's shirt sleeve. Even from ten yards away he could clearly see the man had a Navy SEAL trident tattoo on his bicep.

Fuck!

He'd been one of theirs, and he'd been part of this heinous operation. It made Zed sick.

"Check 'em all," Gray bit out. "I want to know if there are any more Budweiser tats."

On the third man Zed checked, he found a screaming eagle tattoo. "Got us Airborne over here," he hollered.

"Those of you not doing triage, huddle up. Dex, I need you on me," Gray shouted loud enough so Dex could hear even though he was in the hut with the Brockman's.

Dex came out of the hut and glanced around until he spotted Aiden. "O'Malley, Brockman isn't doing well. He's having trouble breathing. I'm pretty sure one of his ribs punctured a lung."

"Give me another minute," Aiden said.

Zed watched as he finished applying a tourniquet to Mrs. Hoff's leg. He gave her a shot, probably full of painkillers and antibiotics. She was going to need to be carried out of the jungle. Zed headed over to Gray and the rest of the team.

"Mister," the girl called out as Zed passed her.

Zed stopped. "Honey, is your name Christie or Debbie?"

"I'm Debbie."

"Well Debbie, I haven't forgotten about Marcia, I promise."

"Raymond's evil. You've got to help her." Her eyes were bright with tears, but this time, she was holding them back.

The picture of Marcia Price filled his consciousness, but instead of the smile on her picture, her face was a mask of dread. "We'll help her. That's what we do," Zed said grimly. He watched as Debbie relaxed. He patted her on the shoulder, then continued on toward Gray and the others.

"…all the communications deciphered ASAP. I need every little bit of data you can get, not just about the bidders, but anything you can find out about who else might be running this op." Dex nodded at Gray then headed toward the barracks.

Gray turned his attention back to the other men gathered around him. "Dalton, I want you to scan all of these assholes fingerprints. Something tells me more than just these two are US Spec Ops. Wyatt, I want you to confiscate all of their personal belongings, we're taking it all. I don't want one damn thing that can be traced back to the U.S. or any other country, for that matter, in case we can't arrange an extraction team for the bodies before someone else stumbles across them."

Aiden walked up to the huddle. "How bad is it?" Gray asked.

"We have two who need immediate help and will need to be carried. The professor and her husband can walk, but they'll be slow like the Brockman girls. Mr. Hoff should be able to assist us with them."

Zed watched Gray carefully. This was the first time he had to see him deal with a totally fucked up situation. It would be interesting to see how he differed from his own lieutenant. "But we don't have everyone accounted for, do we?" Gray asked. "Where's Marcia Price?"

And with that question, Zed decided Gray ranked up there with Max Hogan, the lieutenant of Night Storm. Both men had eyes in the back of their heads.

Aiden pointed to Zed, "He knows what's going on with Marcia. He found one of the Brockman daughters, and she's been begging him to go after the Price girl."

"Tell me what's going on," Gray demanded of Zed.

"When I found Debbie Brockman over near the latrine, she was hiding. She'd been hit in the head by an asshole named Raymond. She said he's evil, and he has Marcia."

"Do we know why he took her?" Gray asked.

"She told me more when I was treating her," Aiden said. "This guy called Marcia an insurance policy. He also said that as long as he had her, he was assured a payoff."

"Most of the targets took head shots, but not the SEAL, I want everyone to take a look at him, and see if we can identify him," Gray said pointing to the corpse. Zed hoped he couldn't. He didn't want to think any man he had served with was capable of throwing his honor away. "Actually, take a look at everyone," Gray corrected himself.

Everyone let Aiden go first, so he could get back to his patients. He made quick work of looking at the men. "Nada," he said as he passed Gray heading into the hut with Harold Brockman. Everybody else made the same loop. Zed was last. He had another feeling, and when he looked down, he was right. The SEAL's name was Sommers. They'd been at Jump School together down at Benning. He'd served on another team in Virginia. There'd been rumblings about him. Nothing that ever bubbled up to command, but rumblings about gambling and a couple of ex-wives.

"I've got a lock on him, Lieutenant. He was on one of the Virginia teams. Do we have time to make a call? If I can get ahold of my communications guy for Night Storm, he'll have the four-one-one on this guy."

"Why's that important?" Gray asked.

"I want to know if this guy Raymond who has Marcia is a SEAL."

Gray tilted his head toward Dex. "Dex, set him up to make his call."

Dex was already standing with the satellite phone in his hand. "Here you go."

It took a moment for Zed to remember Kane McNamara's number since he had him programmed into his phone and didn't have to dial it, but finally, he pulled it out of his memory banks and placed the call. After five rings, a disgruntled Kane answered the phone.

"Who's this?"

"It's Zed. I need info now."

"It's nice to hear from you too. I'm doing fine. Yes, the team misses you."

"Cut the crap," Zed growled. "Get to your fucking computer."

"I'm here now. Ask your questions."

Zed began to breathe a little easier. Dex was a nice guy, but he knew Kane's capabilities, and the man was a fucking wizard. He could pull information out of thin air.

"I need information about a guy named Sommers."

"Fuck, Zed, are you talking about the guy from Phantom Phoenix? I don't need to go to my computer for that. He's a loser. His lieutenant got rid of him. Made it so goddamn hard on him, the bastard ended up quitting."

"Do you have any idea when that was? Do you know what happened to him afterward? Did he have an associate named Raymond?"

He heard Kane sigh. "It was three years ago in August. I remember because we were on that mission in Honduras, and Phoenix was supposed to act as back-up. But the rest of that shit I'm actually going to have to do a little digging, how soon do you need it?"

"Now."

"Hold on." He watched as Hunter, Wyatt, and Dalton started to drag the corpses into the barracks. Meanwhile, Dex was on his comp, reporting into command. Griff came out of a hut leading a woman who was hunched over. The woman had won a Nobel Peace Prize in physics and this slime had roughed her up? He shut his eyes for a moment and whispered a prayer. He'd like to say he couldn't believe it, but he could. It was as if she felt his eyes on him. She looked over at him and gave him a small smile and nod. The mind boggled how sometimes the delineation between good and bad was so clear.

Griff gently settled her next to the Hoffs, so Aiden would eventually be able to look her over. The fact he was still in with Brockman was not a good sign.

"Okay, I have the info, and you're not going to like it," Kane's voice was tense. "Fuck, I don't like it." Zed's gut clenched. Kane never sounded upset. He was the most easygoing guy on the Night Storm team. This did not bode well.

"Tell me."

"Felix Raymond made it through BUD/S third in his class. Hell, I have a copy of his file, there are notes up the ass about what a great SEAL he'll be. That's what makes the next part so bad."

"What?"

"The night before the graduation ceremony, he was charged with murdering his girlfriend in San Diego. The public defender got him off."

"Did he do it?"

"Oh, yeah, he did it, they got him off on a technicality. He's a real piece of work, I'm looking at the psych profile they did on him. They're saying he's a sociopath."

Zed recalled Marcia's picture. He had to go after them.

"How is he connected to Sommers?" Zed asked.

"It looks like he and Sommers went to work for an outfit called Thorn International, basically another security firm that augments our troops, but they both left five months ago."

"Kane, we have an issue here in Borneo. I'm going to hand this over to Dex Evans, he'll fill you in. We need you to keep digging. I don't think we know all the players yet, and we have to know them. I pray to God Raymond's reporting to someone, so he'll want to keep the girl he's holding hostage in good shape."

Zed slammed the phone against Dex's chest, then stormed over to Gray. "I need to go after the Price girl and Raymond."

Gray gave him an assessing look. "What did you find out?"

"Raymond passed BUD/S but didn't get any further because of a murder charge. He went to work for Thorn International, it's a—"

"I know Thorn," Gray interrupted. "Did Raymond do the murder?"

"According to Kane, he was guilty but got off due to a technicality. He's a sociopath. It's worse because he killed his girlfriend, and now, he has a woman as a hostage. I'm hoping there are more players than just these assclowns," Zed said as he waved his hand around the clearing.

"Brockman said a man named Kyle was the supposed leader, but he overheard him checking in with someone else. There's a good chance there was someone outside of the jungle handling the money," Gray informed him.

"Right now, Raymond thinks he has one of Brockman's daughters, someone of value. He can't ever know that isn't true."

"Let's go talk to Brockman," Gray said.

Zed didn't want to, he didn't want to waste another second when he could be following Raymond and getting Marcia out of that madman's hands. He *needed* to do that.

"Zed," Gray said sharply. "Brockman will have information we need."

He nodded and walked swiftly to the hut. Aiden was bent over a prone older man who was obviously pissed.

"Stop fucking around. I'm fine. Where is my daughter, Debbie? Where is Marcia? I won't ask you again." It wasn't often a man who was lying in the dirt could sound so commanding, but what else would you expect from one of the former top officials of the United States Intelligence branches?

"Debbie was hit in the head with the muzzle of a gun," Gray said. Brockman's head whipped around to glare at him. "My second in command, who is our medic, has determined she has a concussion. The less movement she does right now, the better."

"Take me to her."

"After I get your ribs bound," Aiden said grimly. "You're just going to be a detriment to us if we don't get you taken care of."

"You're right," Brockman said in a resigned tone. "What about Marcia?"

"Why don't you go visit with your sister," Gray suggested to the young girl who was holding her father's hand. Brockman immediately caught on.

"Christie, go check on Debbie. Tell her I'm all right, okay?" She bent down and hugged her father's neck. Zed watched as his jaw tightened with the pain, but he still put his arms around his daughter. Obviously giving her comfort was his first priority.

"Are you going to be all right?" she whispered.

"Fit as a fiddle," he promised her. "Now go see your sister."

All four men watched as the girl left the hut. As soon as she was gone, Brockman turned on Gray. "Report," he commanded, his eyes flashing.

"Zed, you got the intel, you give the Director a summary," Gray commanded.

Zed turned to the older man. "When we attacked, Marcia and Debbie were at the latrine with Raymond. According to Debbie, Marcia saved her from being taken as a hostage or getting shot. Instead, Marcia convinced Raymond to take her."

Brockman's fist pounded the dirt. "Raymond was the worst of the bunch," Brockman said grimly. "I'm eternally grateful to Marcia for intervening." He jabbed his finger in the air at Zed. "Now you fucking find her."

He nodded. "I will," Zed promised but didn't move.

"What?" Brockman demanded.

"There's more."

"Tell me."

"Raymond was in the Navy. He passed BUD/S with flying colors."

Brockman's expression turned even grimmer. "I hear a 'but'."

"But the night of graduation, he murdered his girlfriend. His lawyer got him off on a technicality."

"Fuck. When was this?"

"Eight years ago, Sir. Since then, he has been working on assignments with Thorn International. One of the men who is dead out in the clearing was a SEAL as well. He and Raymond were both working for Thorne but quit five months ago."

Brockman frowned. "Five months ago?"

"Yeah, why? Is that significant?" Gray asked.

Brockman pressed two fingers against his eyebrow, his stress evident. "It could be. How many others out there were our men?"

"So far, we've only identified one other. We've taken fingerprints of the rest and scanned them into command. Right now, getting you to safety is our number one priority," Gray answered.

"But if you have information that could explain why we have a bunch of US Spec Ops taking you and your family hostage, you need to let us know."

"I'm running some things off the books right now. You need a top-secret clearance to be briefed on the scope."

Zed and Gray mirrored one another as they crossed their arms over their broad chests.

"With all due respect—" Zed began.

"Of course, I'm going to tell you," Brockman bit out. "I'm just trying to get my thoughts together. I should never have allowed your man O'Malley to give me something for the pain." Brockman was clearly pissed.

Zed relaxed.

"In no way could this ever be traced back to the US, it had to have total deniability. We know but haven't been able to prove the Peaceful Kingdom Brotherhood in Malaysia is funneling funds to ISIS."

"Shit. Doesn't that cult have over one hundred fifty thousand members?" Zed asked.

"You're not keeping up," Gray sighed. "That was last year, it has to have grown by at least ten thousand since then."

"His membership is nearing two hundred thousand," Brockman corrected. "Afiq Zikri is like the Pied Piper, he's getting Muslims and non-Muslims to join. Hell, there are centers popping up in places in the United States."

"And you think he's funding ISIS?" Gray asked.

"Not just that. We're working on infiltrating his inner circle because we're pretty sure he's also tapping his most zealous recruits to join ISIS."

"Meanwhile, we've got people around the world thinking he's a cross-between Martin Luther King Jr. and Mahatma Gandhi," Zed said with disgust. Then he peered over at Brockman. "Are you working with Thorne for this?"

"Just peripherally. For the most part, they are too ham-handed."

"What else are you working on? Or were working on, the thing that made you wince?" Gray asked.

"We had two ops, one that turned into a real goatfuck, and the other is still on-going. You heard about the prince's palace in Saudi Arabia that was bombed?"

Zed and Gray looked at one another, then nodded.

"That happened on our watch. The Saudis had pulled almost one hundred thousand Yemen nationals visas and sent them back home. Hell, they'd been working in Saudi Arabia for years, sending money home, then suddenly they were without jobs, and forced back to their country that had no jobs waiting for them. What did they do? They joined Al-Qaeda. Who were they mad at? The Saudis. That's how the Thorne Group got involved."

"Explain," Gray said.

"Off the books, we helped the Saudis employ the Thorne Group to put security in place. My job was to keep the Saudis and Thorne informed of imminent and credible threats. We helped them foil at least forty different Al-Qaeda attacks."

It didn't matter. Failure was never an option. He looked at Brockman and saw he lived by that motto as well.

"So that happened six months ago, right?" Gray said.

Brockman nodded.

"How many Thorne casualties?"

"Seventeen," Brockman answered immediately. Yep, just as Zed suspected, Brockman took this personally.

"Did the people at Thorne know you were involved?" Zed asked.

"Just ownership. But if someone good really wanted to dig, I'm sure they could have found out," Brockman sighed.

"And the last op?" Gray asked.

"This can't be what it's about. It just came about four weeks ago." Brockman's voice trailed off.

"What?" Zed demanded.

"Three weeks ago, Kyle and his men were selected to guard the yacht."

"What's the op?"

"Fissionable material was stolen from France."

"Where's it going? North Korea? Pakistan?" Gray asked.

Brockman gave both men a grim look. "Our source says Turkey."

"Holy fuck," Zed breathed out. "Are you sure?"

"No. But this source has been one hundred percent right for ten years. That's why we're following the material, instead of just reacquiring it. If someone in Turkey has gone rogue, we need to know about it."

Zed thought about it. After Russia took over the Crimean peninsula and Turkey's proximity to Iraq, he could see where factions within the country would think having a nuclear arsenal would be critical.

"You're getting it," Brockman nodded to him.

"Yeah," Zed agreed. "I'm getting it, but I'm not liking it."

"Why you? Why not have the C.I.A. work on this?" Gray asked.

"Plausible deniability. They need some distance on all of these ops in case they go south. But I'm using some of their people when needed."

"So, these people who wanted you could have known about your involvement with current operations and wanted information on them, right?" Gray said.

"Yes."

"Or they could have just been after you because you were the former NSA Director and wanted you, thinking you had knowledge of your previous job."

Brockman nodded. "This is a fucking mess."

"We need to find out who Kyle really was and who he was working for," Gray said.

"Let's hope they wanted you for your current stuff," Zed said.

Brockman raised an eyebrow in question.

"Getting info on that shit is a hell of a lot more valuable to someone than some old shit you might have done at the NSA. That means they have more incentive to keep Marcia alive and use her as leverage over you." Zed said.

"You're right," Brockman agreed. "So, who's going after her?"

"I am," Zed immediately responded.

Gray gave Zed a considering look, then turned to Brockman. "He'll find her and bring her to safety."

"I'm sure your Zed's good. But you don't understand, this Raymond, there's something *wrong* with him. Can you spare two men?" Brockman asked.

"Zed will bring her back," Gray said again.

Brockman pushed himself up the side of the hut, the only outward sign of pain were the beads of sweat that dripped down his temples. "How bad is it, Lieutenant? Are we going to be able to evacuate? I can make it with limited assistance."

"No, Sir, you can't," Gray stated emphatically. "Neither can two others. We also have your daughters we're concerned about. With all of you, this should take us about three days to get to the road that leads to the coast. There will be a helicopter evac there to take us to the USS Ronald Reagan."

"And Marcia?"

"I'll make sure she is taken to the Reagan as well," Zed said with quiet assurance.

"I know she isn't my daughter, but I think of her like one of my own. She's special, Son."

Zed looked the man dead in the eye. "I know." He turned to Gray, "I need to go coordinate with Dex, and see if Kane has any more intel."

Gray nodded.

CHAPTER THREE

Marcia couldn't catch her breath.

"Faster." Raymond yanked on the rope that was tied around her wrists. He liked doing that. Even when she was keeping up, he would jerk the rope, just so she would stumble. What a needle dick. That was probably his problem. Raymond was such an A-hole because he had a teeny tiny penis.

"Keep up, we're on a deadline."

Marcia kept her head down, so she could watch for branches and anything else on the jungle floor she might stumble over. She was so tired, but she would never admit it. She'd done track in high school, and she jogged every other day at home. She was never going to give up even though her wrists were raw from the rope, and her hands were scraped and battered from when she'd fallen.

"What do you mean we're on a deadline?" she asked. One thing she had learned spending time with Mr. B., knowledge was power.

Thank God, he went around a fallen tree instead of climbing over it. "You don't think Kyle was the brains of this operation, do you? Fuck, he couldn't run a Burger King. Look how things ended up. I was always working with the big guy behind Kyle's back. I made sure I had a contingency plan. I was smart."

"I don't know Raymond, seeing as we're on the run, you're not looking too smart. I think you would have been lucky just to be working the fryer at the Burger King."

He yanked the rope, and she had just a second to see the rage on his face and feel the spittle hit her as he roared, "Bitch." She tried to duck his hand, but he was too fast. Stars exploded, and she hit the ground.

Her nose was smashed into the damp jungle floor. Her mouth tasted like copper, dirt, and the pungent bitter taste of leaves filled her mouth. She spit, trying to clear her mouth. She didn't know how long she was on the ground before more pain seared through her scalp. Raymond pulled her hair even harder as he lifted her head.

"Drink this."

He shoved the straw from his Camelback into her mouth, so she could gulp down some water. As she was drinking he talked. "You shouldn't have been so stupid. If you hadn't mouthed off, I wouldn't have had to hit you."

Raymond pulled her up into a sitting position. Marcia touched the side of her face with her fingers. She glared at the douche-nozzle, but just squinting her eyes at him hurt.

"Don't push your luck, Lesley. What I put up with in camp won't fly out here. Women don't walk all over me. I only allowed it before because I didn't need the hassle. But make no mistake, women need to know their place. You get me?"

He coiled the rope around his hand and Marcia saw the fanatical glee in his face. She had no doubt in her mind if he didn't have some kind of need for her, she'd be dead. And it wouldn't be an easy death. This boy had serious mommy issues. Marcia bowed her head, so he couldn't see her expression, she knew her eyes would give her away.

"I understand. I'm sorry, Raymond. Please forgive me," she said softly.

That apology left a worse taste in her mouth than the jungle floor.

He pulled her to her feet and put his face close to hers. His breath reeked. "Just make sure it doesn't happen again."

She nodded, keeping her eyes downward. Her head hurt really bad, and she felt dizzy. Trying to maintain this subservient façade was going to be tough when she felt like crap, but darn-it she could do what she needed to in order to live through this crappy hand life had dealt her.

She'd known Mr. Brockman almost all of her life. Her family had lived across the street from his family when her parents had been alive. Mr. B. would send those soldiers after her. There was no way he'd leave her hanging in the wind. She just needed to hold on and not let her mouth get her killed.

"Can I ask a question?" she asked meekly.

"Can you be pleasant?"

"I promise," she said in a low voice. "You said we were on a deadline. How fast do we need to go?"

The look he gave her made her skin crawl. "As soon as I get to a phone, I'll get in touch with Jefferies and see what plans he might have for you. If it's worth my while, I'll turn you over to him. If not," he shrugged. "If not, you and I are going to do a bit of Skyping with your father. I have a bone to pick with him."

"What do you mean we'll Skype?" Marcia hated the tremor she heard in her voice.

Raymond pulled her even closer to him and she could see bits of food stuck between his teeth. "Pray hard, Lesley, pray really hard Jefferies can make it worth my while to hand you over because your daddy has a lot to answer for. I want him to suffer for my friends who died." He shoved her away from him, then smiled brightly like they were at a cocktail party. "But don't you worry about it, I'm sure Jefferies will make me rich, and soon, you'll be home in the bosom of your family."

She looked at him in disbelief. How could he change personalities in the blink of an eye?

"Quit staring at me," he growled.

She looked down at the dirt.

"Good girl. Now, let's get going. The sooner I get to a phone, the sooner you'll be home."

Sure, she believed that. Just like she believed in leprechauns, the Easter bunny, and the tooth fairy. There wasn't a chance in hell they were ever planning on letting her return to the U.S. Marcia took a deep trembling breath.

Get it together Price.

One breath. One moment. One hour. One day. She could get through this.

"Did you hear me, Lesley? You get to go home? So, speed it up."

"Sir, I could go faster if you untied my hands. My balance is off." Gah, she had to swallow down the bile using the word 'Sir', but if it would get him to untie her hands…

"Nice try. Suck it up, Girly," he said as he yanked at the rope. "If you keep up, I'll feed you the next time I need to take a piss."

Her stomach growled at the mention of food. She'd keep up. Her foot hit water. What in the world?

"Where are we?" she asked before she could stop herself.

"We just hit the swamps leading up to the river. Nobody's going to be able to track us through this shit."

Marcia whimpered as her Sketchers sunk into the mud and tried to suck her shoe off when she lifted it back out. How was she going to keep up now? He had boots on. This was going to be impossible.

"Raymond."

His eyes cut to hers, and he glared.

"What is it?"

"Can we stop while I tie my shoes on tighter? They won't stay on in this mud."

"For fuck's sake, you should have worn something more practical," he reprimanded harshly.

She bit her tongue just in time. How stupid was he to say something like that? As if she had thought she was going to be kidnapped off the yacht. He stopped next to a rotted stump. He lifted her up like she weighed nothing. The show of strength gave her the heebie-jeebies. He scraped the stinking mud off her shoes, so he could get to her shoelace. Two beetles crawled over her jean covered leg. She whimpered.

"Don't be a pussy," Raymond said as he crushed the bugs into the fabric of her jeans. Once again, she felt herself throw-up in her mouth and was forced to swallow it back down. The fetid and sour taste made her eyes water.

"Quit your crying." She looked down at the orange smears on her pants and winced at the tightness of her shoes, but it was for the best. Of course, it was nothing compared to the pain in her face. Marcia had never been hit before in her life, and she'd like to avoid it in the future. What's more, if she got another injury, it would just make it tougher for her to ride out this nightmare. He hit the side of her hip. "Up and at 'em. We're burning daylight."

Raymond plucked her off the stump and dropped her into the murky water of the swamp. This time he put an arm around her shoulder. "Can't afford to have you fall face first and drown, so you're next to me."

Marcia knew she was pushing her luck, but she had to try. "Raymond?" she said meekly.

"Now what?"

"I'd really like to put my arm around you, so I could hang on better. I really don't want to drown. You know I can't get away from you. You're too fast and strong. Can you please untie me? I'm begging you. Please?"

As he stood there looking down at her, she gave a pleading smile, all the time thinking how nice it would be to kick him in the balls.

"You're right. You can't get away from me." He plucked a wicked looking knife from its sheath and cut the rope from her wrists. "Okay, baby, cuddle up. The faster we get to a phone, the sooner we can determine what your fate is."

* * *

Zed went to talk to Dex. Could it get any worse? As soon as he thought those words, he winced. Damned right he was superstitious, he came by it naturally. And Dex's expression was going to prove him right, he just knew it.

"Come look at the screen," Dex said pointing to his small laptop that could damn near withstand a nuclear attack.

"Our boys, Raymond and Sommers were involved in that mission you told Kane and me about with the Saudi palace. There were only five survivors, and they were two of them."

"So, they have an ax to grind with Brockman," Zed said grimly.

"Only if they knew he was behind the scenes," Dex said carefully. "There's still the fact Kyle got everyone together immediately after the fissionable material was stolen from France."

"You and Kane need to work that shit out. I'm going after Marcia, it's already been two hours. I'll take the comm with me, and you can feed me any information you get."

"To be on the safe side, Gray wants you to take one of the satellite phones," Dex said as he handed it to Zed. "For all we know, there'll be a damn meteor shower or some such shit that'll screw up the comm."

That had really happened, so Zed took the satellite phone. "You need to get more information from Brockman about the mission in Saudi."

"Agreed," Dex nodded.

"Good." Zed gave him a chin tilt and headed toward the spot where Debbie had said Raymond and Marcia had disappeared into the jungle. It was easy to spot where they'd entered, the foliage was trampled. He adjusted his pack and started out a jog. He intended to catch up with them in less than four hours, he didn't give a shit if they had a two-hour head start. With Marcia as a hostage, he knew he could easily catch up.

Zed paused at different points.

"Fuck," he breathed out under his breath. He could see where someone had fallen. It was a small body, obviously Marcia. He carefully examined the fall pattern and noted her hands hadn't spread out like they should of. If he had to make an educated guess, Raymond had tied her hands in front of her. He hated the thought of it, but the pragmatic part of him knew that was going to make it easier to catch up with them since she couldn't go as fast.

It was another half mile when he saw another major disturbance in the jungle floor. It was another indent that was the size of a woman, not a man. He inspected it and this time he saw blood on the leaves. "Goddammit." He brushed aside the leaves, looking for some kind of rock that might account for her to be bleeding. He didn't find anything but the spongy rot of leaves. That left only one explanation, she was bleeding before she hit the ground. "Fucker!" He'd done something to bloody her. Zed felt his fists clench and unclench.

This time when he sprang up from his crouch, he started moving even faster, then had to force himself to slow down. He knew better. The last thing he needed to do was injure himself. Taking a calming breath, he skirted a large fallen tree and continued following their trail.

The jungle started to thin out, and he saw a flat wide expanse before him. It was a swamp. It reminded him of his time training on the Pearl River in Mississippi. Zed was from the streets of LA, he'd hated the swamp training. Abso-fucking-lutely hated it.

"Suck it up, Zaragoza," he muttered. He flipped his rifle down behind his back and crouched down and tied his boots on as tight as possible. It was only going to help him for the first half mile, he knew it, the damn silt and mud was going to get into his boots and then slide between his toes. Out of all of his training, trudging through the swamp was the one he hated the most. One of his teammates was from Louisiana, and he never stopped giving Zed shit.

"Well, Cullen, you sure as hell would be laughing your ass off if you could see me now," Zed said with a half-smile. Then his features turned grim. The problem was there was no good way to track them in the shallow water which he damn well knew was Raymond's intent. He'd be heading for the coast, most likely down the Kinabatangan river since he'd headed inland.

Zed took his first long strides into the swamp while hitting the comm device.

"Dex? You read me?"

"Gotcha. Where you at?"

"Headed toward the Kinabatangan river. Managed to find me some swampland."

Zed heard a chuckle come through the line, and it wasn't Dex.

"Your favorite," Kane said. Shit, somehow Dex had conferenced in his teammate from Night Storm.

"It's not on the map. There shouldn't be a swamp," Zed grumbled.

"I'm going to tell Cullen," Kane laughed.

"Tell him later. Have you figured out which angle Raymond is working? Or who he might be working with?" Zed questioned.

"Nada," Kane said, all laughter gone from his voice. "If Raymond is really heading toward that river, you gotta know it eventually spits out near Sandakan near the tip of Borneo."

"He's going to have to hijack a boat," Zed thought aloud. He looked down at his GPS. There was a spot with a significant bend in the river. He mentioned it to Kane and Dex.

"Yep, that would be the perfect place to ambush someone," Dex agreed.

"I'm heading there," Zed stated. "Do you know what kind of boats I can expect on the river?" he asked.

"I've researched," Kane said. "It's mostly locals. Some longboats, kayaks, canoes, and houseboats."

"Okay." Zed looked off into the distance, thinking it through. He saw a swarm of brightly colored birds fly by and monkeys chattering in the distance. He felt himself calm. He had a plan. "Thanks. This helped," he told the two men. "How's it going with the rescue?" he asked Dex.

There was a pause.

"Tell me," Zed prompted.

"Brockman's not doing well. His right lung is deflated. We had to fashion a stretcher and wrap him in so that he wouldn't jostle his rib and do more damage."

"Shit you're close enough to Brunei, can't they help?" Kane asked.

"The jungle is too dense. We have to just wait until we get to that road. We need about eighteen more hours. Gray just decided to have Hunter and I camp with the others while the rest of the team double-time it to the chopper evac site."

"How quick do you think you can make it to an extraction point?" Kane asked.

"They think they can make it in half the time while still keeping him relatively stable. He needs surgery, and they can provide that on the Reagan."

"Gotcha," Kane said. "In the meantime, I'm going to have my eye on you Zed. If you get off track, I'll ping you."

"Steak dinner says I won't."

"I'm not taking that bet," Kane chuckled again. "But I'll have your back, anyway."

"You always do," Zed muttered as he snagged a good-sized branch that was floating in the murky water. "Okay, ladies, gotta go."

He pushed the branch into the mud ahead of him, making sure that there weren't any drop-offs. It shouldn't slow him down, and it would save him a dunking. Cullen would be so proud.

CHAPTER FOUR

Marcia had been trying to get away from Raymond for hours. Not to escape. She knew that was hopeless in the swamp, but she just wanted his arm *off* her.

Suck it up, Price. Your life is on the line, and you're over here caring if he has his arm around your waist? She shuddered because his fingers gripped her stomach, making her want to throw up. Marcia couldn't help her visceral reaction, but seriously, this should just be number forty-one on her list of things that were bothering her. She tried to concentrate on the fact she was probably going to be sold to the highest bidder and tortured.

Torture was less intimate though, right?

God, Price, you are a piece of work.

"Where are we going?" she asked Raymond when he stopped and looked down at his hand-held GPS device.

"Thought you weren't talking to me, Girly," Raymond looked down at her with a sly grin.

"Figure since this concerns my life, I should pretend to care."

He gave her a long considering look. Oh crappola, had she come off too flip? She really didn't want to be hit again. She'd forgotten she needed to be acting subservient. Acting like a doormat needed to be number one on her list. As soon as she thought that, her mind rebelled. Absolutely not. Her number one priority was to survive. Life was too precious not to do everything possible to fight and stay alive. So, no more smart-mouth.

"I'm sorry Raymond, I'm just getting a little tired, so I was wondering how much longer before we get where we're going."

"Days. But we'll take a break at nightfall. Do you need more water?"

She shook her head. If she had water, she'd need to pee. She didn't want to have to do that here in the marsh with him looking on.

He shoved the device into his backpack, this time wrapping his arm around her shoulders. "Let's go. Should only be about two more miles, then lucky for you, we won't have to walk anymore."

Marcia sloshed through the water, grateful he had at least shortened his stride, so she could more easily keep up. She looked down at the muddy water, wondering if there were snakes in it. She was so tired. It took all of her energy just to put one foot in front of the other. She thought about Christie,

Debbie, and their father, and her stomach turned over. She sent up fervent prayers all of them would be okay.

Who were the men who had come to their rescue? Would they be able to assist Mr. B.? He'd been trying to hide it, but Marcia had known his injuries had been bad. He'd been having trouble breathing.

"What?"

It took a moment for her to realize that Raymond was talking to her.

"Huh?"

"You were mumbling. I wanted to know what you were saying."

Marcia realized two things, the water was only as deep as a mud puddle, and Raymond was squeezing her shoulder tightly as he glared down at her.

"I was praying," she finally answered honestly.

He barked out a laugh.

"What a waste of time. God isn't going to save you. You need to pray to your new god, and that would be me."

"I was saying prayers for," she stopped herself before she called Harold Brockman, Mr. B. "I was praying for my dad and my sisters. Do you think they're okay?"

"You better be praying for your dad's safety. He's the one who's going to have to get you out of this."

"What do you mean?" Marcia asked carefully. She didn't want to give away the fact that she was excited to get information from Raymond. What did this man Jefferies want her for?

"You're pretty enough but selling a white woman into the sex trade only gets me so much. I'm looking for a hell of a lot bigger pay off than that."

Marcia stumbled.

"Bitch, keep walking, we still have a long way to go."

Pull it together Price, she admonished herself. Protecting the girls from the human trafficking had always been on her mind ever since they'd been kidnapped, so why get her panties in a twist now? She needed to keep herself together.

"Don't like the sound of that, do you?" Raymond laughed. He pulled her along, so they were walking again. "Come on, Lesley, one foot in front of the other, don't make me have to carry your ass, it'll just make me angry."

"I don't want to make you angry." Boy, wasn't that the truth. Her face still hurt. "But what do you mean Dad can get me out of this? We're not all that rich."

"Rich is a relative term. Once I can get to a phone, I'll be able to negotiate a price that will make me rich."

"With Jefferies? What will they do with me? I thought you said if you gave me to him, I could go home?" Marcia couldn't stop the rapid-fire questions from shooting out of her mouth.

Raymond squeezed her neck. "You're kind of cute when you get all cat curious. It won't hurt to tell you the ways of the world. You know the old deal we had in place. Sell you, your sisters, and your dad to the highest bidder. Then let that bidder do whatever the fuck they wanted to you and your sisters while Daddy-dear watched until he confessed everything he knew."

Marcia hadn't been able to think of anything else for days. It was the reason she hadn't been able to hold down food.

"I was always behind that plan because that meant that your dad would suffer. Like he made my friends suffer and die."

"What are you talking about?" Marcia demanded as she struggled to pull her right foot out of a deeper hole of mud.

"Your father fucked up last year when he provided intel on one of his projects. He only had one fucking job, and that was to determine when those Al-Qaeda fucks were going to show up. He screwed up on the time. He told us in absolute terms they would arrive at ten p.m. They showed up at three p.m. and seventeen good men died because of his fuck-up."

"What are you talking about?" Marcia wanted information, but she knew she needed to act ignorant too. She'd been living at the Brockman's house since Mrs. B. died, so she could help watch over Christie and Debbie. She wasn't stupid. She knew that Mr. B. still had his hands in a lot of different pots even though he'd retired. In some ways, she guessed, he had even more freedom to get things done, and he was making the most of it. She wondered what project had gone so terribly wrong that seventeen men had died.

"What? You can't believe your dad got good men slaughtered? Well, he did."

"Are you telling me he was working with men like you? Mercenaries?"

"Don't get up on your high horse. Before I took this project, I was working for the Thorne Group. I came over to the dark-side so I could help take your daddy down and also for the money. It was a twofer."

"So, it was men from the Thorne Group who died? They were working with Dad?"

"Yep."

"How are you going to make this deal work now that you just have me?"

Raymond's stride faltered, but he immediately continued on as if nothing had happened. "That's the part where I need the phone. Your daddy always has little operations going on throughout the world, and Jefferies is the man in the know. Those operations your daddy handles cost a shit-ton of off-the-books money. He'll just have to slide some over our way if he wants his pretty daughter back home, now won't he?" Raymond grinned down at her evilly.

Marcia kept quiet for a long while, using the sounds and the scents of the swamp to block out the feel of Raymond's hands on her body. She was jarred out of her reverie when Raymond suddenly stopped and pulled out his GPS device.

"Thank fuck. We're almost to the river. Just another quarter mile, and we'll be at the river bend. If you're really quiet, you should be able to hear the rushing water."

They were both silent. She looked up and saw all the trees in the distance. She could hear the monkeys and the sound of water. Marcia looked at her mud-caked feet with dread. The man could say whatever he wanted about Mr. B. paying for her return, but that was never going to happen if Raymond had his way. He wanted Mr. B. to suffer, and that meant Marcia was going to have to suffer.

"Do you hear it?" he asked her.

"Oh yeah. Everything is coming through loud and clear."

* * *

"Fuck. Fuck. Fuck." Zed said the words in a low whisper. Dammit, if he'd only gotten out of the camp twenty minutes sooner, he would have caught up with Raymond and Marcia. Now they were on some damn boat they'd hijacked, headed down river. The only, and he meant *only* good thing he could see out of this was there wasn't a body in the water or on the shore.

Pull it back, Zaragoza. He looked closer at the disturbance at the shoreline. He could see where the boat had actually flattened a lot of reeds, but he didn't see any evidence of the plants having been cut or chewed by motor blades. He took a deep breath and gave a slight smile. So, the boat was probably being propelled by good old-fashioned paddle power. Or it could just be that the motor hadn't been turned on.

He needed a boat, and he needed one now. Preferably one with a motor. He clicked his comm, and didn't get a signal to Dex, so he dug out the satellite phone.

"I need help," he said to Dex without preamble.

"I'm conferencing in Kane," was Dex's immediate response.

Zed waited until he heard a click.

"You all here?" Dex asked. Zed and Kane said yes at the same time.

"I'm at the river." Zed started. "Really fresh tracks are telling me Raymond and Marcia just confiscated a boat to head downriver. They probably have a twenty to thirty-minute head start." Zed knew he sounded pissed, but that's because he was pissed. "I can't see them," he continued. "How much boat traffic can I expect? Am I close to civilization? Do you think I should head out after them on foot and hope they camp come nightfall?"

"Here's what you need to know," Kane said in a calm voice. "You're currently ten miles up-river from where the Eco-Tourism really starts on the river. So, you're going to have to figure out a way to either stay out of sight or blend in, and you're going to have a hell of a time blending in with your rifle," Kane said.

Dex laughed and Zed felt relief wash over him. This was workable.

"Why are you laughing, Dex?" Kane asked.

"I'm hurt Kane, I leave for nine weeks, and you forget who you're dealing with," Zed said.

There was a long pause, and then Kane laughed. "So, you scrounged up some civvies before heading out?"

"Now, I'm offended. Of course not. Wyatt's low man on the totem pole. I had him do it."

Dex laughed even harder.

"I'll be able to blend in, I have an extra duffel to shove the SCAR into because I'm sure as hell not leaving my rifle behind."

"That could work," Kane relented. "Now, to answer your question. Where you're currently at, you're probably going to run into mostly locals. There are fishermen and people who live on houseboats. Sometimes, out where you are, you'll have folks hunting orangutans."

Zed could hear the disgust in Kane's voice, but he wasn't quite clear about something.

"What—" Dex started.

"They kill the mother and steal the babies," Kane explained, answering Dex's unanswered question. "People will pay top dollar for their private zoos or to raise them as pets."

"Sounds like Raymond was just lucky to get a boat," Zed said. "I'm going to head down-river and catch up with them when they go ashore for the night."

"Let us know your progress," Dex said.

"You got it."

Zed disconnected and tucked the phone back into his pack and took out his GPS. He wanted to keep track of the distance, so he knew when he was getting close to the Eco-Tourist area. He looked at the clothes Wyatt had found for him in the men's barracks but decided to stay in his mission clothes for the time being. They were a hell of a lot more comfortable that was for damn sure.

He looked up at the sun, just a couple of more hours 'til nightfall. He stayed close to the shoreline but far enough in the foliage, so he wouldn't be spotted if someone was watching the riverbank. Zed's movements were silent as he moved through the jungle, so the birds continued to sing and the monkeys continued to chatter. As he listened, he couldn't help but think about the bastards who would butcher unsuspecting mothers, so they could kidnap baby orangutans.

* * *

Marcia rocked the baby, relieved the child was finally calm. Too bad the same couldn't be said for his mother. She looked over at the small woman who cowered in the corner of the boat. Her eyes were huge as she trembled and stared at Raymond's automatic rifle. Marcia had no idea who the old man was who was lying on the deck. He'd been kind enough to maneuver the boat over to the shore when Marcia had waved him over, but as soon as Raymond had stepped out from behind the tree and boarded the boat, he had tried to fight him. The old man had to be at least seventy, and he went down hard under the butt of Raymond's rifle.

The woman had scrambled over to the old man, trying to revive him. She was crying and moaning in a language Marcia didn't understand. That was when Marcia heard a baby crying. She looked under the houseboat's small awning and saw a crib where a toddler was standing up, their arms out. The child was babbling, and Marcia wasn't sure if it was toddler-speak or the same foreign language the woman was speaking. When the woman didn't go over to the baby, Marcia went over and picked it up.

"What are you doing, Girly?" Raymond demanded.

"Taking care of the baby."

He grunted, sounding like he was agreeing. He grabbed the large paddle the old man had used to get over to them. Raymond then grabbed hold of the same wooden handle the old man had been holding onto. What was the name of it again? It was a rudder or tiller or something like that. Why hadn't she paid attention when she'd gone sailing when her dad and mom were alive?

Raymond got them into the middle of the river, then they started going a lot faster than she thought they would have. Marcia rocked the baby and sidled up to the woman, giving her an encouraging smile, but it was no use, she just sat there holding the old man's head in her lap. So, Marcia decided to concentrate on the baby in her arms. She didn't know if it was a boy or a girl. Instead of thinking of the child as an it, she decided he was a boy. His cloth diaper was wet, and she needed to find a new one. Marcia ducked back under the awning and started to go into the small interior of the houseboat.

"Hey, bitch, where do you think you're going? Stay where I can see you," Raymond roared.

Marcia spun around. She hadn't even thought about Raymond in ten minutes, her entire focus had been on the small family.

"The baby's diaper is wet, I need to get him a new one."

Raymond pointed his gun at the mother. "Get her to do it."

"She's too scared. She won't move," Marcia protested.

"It's her brat. Isn't it instinct?"

"Her husband or father is bleeding, she's trying to help him. Just let me find the diaper," Marcia requested reasonably.

"Okay," Raymond smirked. "I'll hold the baby to make sure you don't do anything funny."

She didn't want to relinquish the baby to him. "You need to steer the boat."

"Only takes one hand. Don't backtalk me." He held out his arm. "The sooner you hand over the brat, the sooner you'll be back. Who knows, you might find something to feed it."

Marcia closed her eyes and said a little prayer, then handed over the baby. She ran to the small little room that held a small little kitchen and two cots. She saw a cooler and found a bottle.

Aaaaa-eeeeee

Marcia stood stalk still at the sound of the ear-splitting terrified shriek, then she bolted outside.

"No!" She screamed as her horrified eyes took in the scene in front of her. Raymond was holding the baby by its feet over the river. The baby was struggling wildly, the mother trying to get to her child as Raymond easily held her off. The mother shoved against him, howling her fright.

"Find what you needed, Girly?" Raymond asked calmly.

It took all of Marcia's willpower to answer in a mild tone. "Yes, I did. But I dropped it when I heard the screaming."

"Well, I guess we'll just have to hope my arm doesn't get tired by the time you get the stuff you need, huh?"

"Why are you doing this? Let me have the baby," Marcia beseeched.

"I think after you get the shit you need, the little mommy will be able to take care of her own kid, don't you? I think she's done being too scared to come out of the corner."

The woman was looking back and forth between Raymond and Marcia. She was sobbing.

"Come on, Lesley, you better go get the bottle and diaper. Better hurry."

Marcia turned and ran. She was back in seconds. "I've got it. Please let the baby go."

Raymond lowered his arm just a little. She knew he did it on purpose just to torture her and the baby's mother. "Please Raymond. I'll do whatever you want. Please don't hurt the baby."

"Lesley, I just want you to do what I say when I say it. Got it?"

"Anything Raymond." Tears flooded her eyes and spilled over. "Please, I'm begging you."

"God, there is nothing prettier than a crying woman." He pulled the baby back over the edge of the boat and shoved the child toward the mother. They collapsed into one another's arms.

"Don't stand there, Lesley, give them the diaper and milk, that's what started all of this. It was your fault it got to this point."

"I'm sorry, Raymond. You're right, it's all my fault," Marcia said as she walked forward. After half a step, she realized what she'd said and meant.

My God, get it together girl. Don't believe his craziness is your fault. You're being manipulated by a madman.

When she looked up into his eyes, she saw his pleasure at her behavior and realized she needed to keep it up, now it wasn't just her life on the line.

Marcia crouched down and attempted to hand the diaper and bottle to the mother, but she wasn't having any of it.

Raymond roared toward them, "Take it, you dumb bitch. Get your kid to stop it's wailing." The mother and baby just started crying louder.

"Raymond, please, I'm begging you. Let me take them under the awning. You'll be able to see us all the time. I'll be able to quiet them down, I promise."

"No!" he shouted into her face, spit flying. "Make them shut up out here."

Marcia turned her head and looked at the mother and baby and saw the futility of Raymond's demand. She changed her position, so she was on her knees, her butt on her heels. She looked down at the deck floor.

"I'm trying to do what you want, Raymond, I really am," she said in a soft voice.

He pinched her chin and yanked her head up, so she met his eyes. "I can't stand their pathetic caterwauling. Make it stop. Make it stop." Marcia's breath stopped when she saw the pistol in his hand.

"You told me you liked it when I cried."

"Your tears make me hard. Their tears are like nails on a chalkboard. If they don't stop soon, I'll kill them."

"I don't want you to have to kill them, Raymond. I don't want that for you," she coaxed. His fingers relaxed slightly. He looked indecisive. "Let me try to calm them down. The baby's hungry, and once I can calm the baby down, the mother will calm down."

"No funny business."

"I promise. I want everybody to come out safe and sound. You know you're holding all the cards."

She watched his sly smile of satisfaction at those words.

Thank God, the submissive crap had worked.

He waved his pistol. "Go, fix this."

On her hands and knees, Marcia crawled over to the mother and child. As soon as she got to them, she wrapped her arms around them.

"It's going to be all right," she murmured in soft tones. She eased up onto her feet, coaxing the mother up with her. "That's right, come with me." She knew the woman couldn't understand her, but her soothing tone must have been getting through. She made sure to keep her body between the woman and Raymond, so hopefully, she couldn't see the crazy man and his gun.

"You're doing so good. Let's get your baby taken care of, shall we? Such a good baby. I bet your baby is going to grow up to be an all-star. I can't wait to find out if he or she is a boy or girl." Marcia kept up the non-sense talking as they made their way under the awning. Some of the tension left the woman's body, and as a result, the toddler wasn't thrashing around as much.

"I wonder what beautiful name you've given this little bundle. I bet I can't pronounce it." Marcia spied the cushy pile of blankets beside the crib and correctly assumed it was the diaper changing area when the woman placed the child down on it.

The mom looked up at her expectantly. When Marcia just stood there, she reached out with one hand. Marcia realized she was holding the cloth diaper. She smiled and handed it over.

"Sorry about that."

She watched as the woman took off the soggy diaper and Marcia finally realized they were dealing with a little girl. Again, Marcia crouched beside the woman and took the soiled diaper from her. The woman pointed toward a bucket, and Marcia placed it inside.

She knelt back down beside the two and pointed toward herself.

Darn, she almost said Marcia. She started again. She patted her chest and said, "Lesley."

The woman's eyes lit up, and she nodded. She pointed to her own chest. "Nurul."

Lesley pointed toward the little girl who was now just hiccupping instead of full-fledged crying. Nurul said "Hana."

"What a beautiful name," Marcia said. She knew the woman wouldn't understand the words, but she figured the sentiment would get through. Then the woman turned slightly, and she surreptitiously pointed toward the man who was unconscious on the deck.

"Adib." She continued to talk quickly in that other language Marcia didn't understand, tears rolling down Nurul's face. As if she could feel her mother's disquiet, Hana immediately started to fuss. Marcia needed to shut this down, otherwise, Raymond was going to get really angry. She pulled Nurul into her arms.

"Shhhh. It's going to be okay." The young mother clutched Marcia's neck as if she were a lifeline. She continued to speak. Marcia stroked her back, telling her everything would be okay even though she knew it was going to take a miracle for it to be true.

"Keep it down over there!" Raymond shouted.

Nurul's body shuddered, and Marcia held her tighter. Marcia glanced over at Hana who was red in the face. She picked up the bottle she'd set down.

"Nurul," Marcia said pulling away from the woman. She showed her the bottle then motioned toward Hana. Slowly the woman nodded. She picked up the cantankerous little girl and sat down cross-legged with the child on her lap. With a little work, the baby took the bottle and Marcia breathed a sigh of relief.

"About goddamned time. Lesley, get over here."

Now what? Marcia wondered. She got up and went over to Raymond, carefully keeping her eyes downward, only looking up through her lashes. The man didn't look angry that was a good sign. When she got within four feet of him, she stopped and waited.

"Get me some food, there has to be something on this godforsaken boat. I want hot food. I'm going to have my rifle aimed at the kid the whole time I can't see you. If you take more than ten minutes, I'm going to shoot the kid. I've killed men and women before, but never a kid. Sounds like a new kind of high point I can rack up, so don't think I'm kidding."

Her eyes flew up to look at his. He chuckled.

"Better get cracking. Don't waste your time trying to tell if I'm serious." He took a step toward her, and his voice lowered. "Because, Girly, I'm fucking serious as a heart attack."

Her blood turned to ice. She couldn't help the whimper that escaped. He shoved her with the muzzle of his rifle, and she stumbled a step backward. "Go. Time's a-wastin'."

Marcia turned and ran toward the little kitchen she'd seen. She ignored it when Nurul called out her name. There was a little metal contraption that had a teapot sitting on top of it. She didn't see any kind of propane tank beside it, but there were matches close by. That had to be what they used to cook on. Marcia felt tears of frustration starting.

"Stop! You can do this." If she could gut a fish and fry it in a pan over an open fire, she could figure this out.

She went to the cooler that wasn't very cool. Good, maybe she could find something in here to poison Raymond with. There were a lot of things she didn't recognize. Eventually, she found three eggs, and that she could work with. They'd been near the bottom where items were colder. So much for poisoning the beast. She also found a baggie full of cooked rice. Good, she could warm that up to go with the scrambled eggs.

She peeked out and saw that Nurul was still feeding Hana, so she wouldn't be any help. Maybe that was for the best, they'd probably be working at cross-purposes in the kitchen, anyway. There was one long thin cupboard, and in there she struck gold. Frying pan, spices, dishes, and cooking oil. Now, she just had to figure out how to light the freaking little stove.

She took off the teapot and replaced it with the skillet. She fiddled with the knob until she heard a hissing sound. She lit a match and prayed. She backed far away, and with just two fingers she touched the match next to the burner. Marcia sighed with relief when a small flame licked upwards. Success!

She poured some cooking oil into the pan and cracked the eggs into the bowl. She soon had scrambled eggs and rice on a plate, no silverware, just chopsticks. Marcia left the galley and made sure she was in front of the mother and child as she walked toward Raymond with his hot food.

"Weren't you damn lucky? You did it with thirty seconds to spare," he grinned. She hated it when he gave a genuine smile, it made her realize he could be charming and good-looking. It scared her to think how many people had failed to see the monster underneath the mask.

"Bitch, get me a fork," he bellowed when she handed him the chopsticks.

"I looked, they only had chopsticks. I'm sorry. Please forgive me."

He put the food on the deck floor. "Go find something for me to drink. I'll have to use my own fork. Hurry back."

He started to shrug off his backpack and Marcia ran toward the galley again. Near the bottom of the cooler, she'd seen a couple of jugs of liquid. She pushed things aside and found the jugs. One was milk, and the other was a light orange color liquid. She took a quick taste. Kind of warm papaya juice. Frantically, she went to the cupboard and looked for glass.

Shazam! Her eyes widened when she spotted the pistol. It looked like it was from World War II, but it still was a gun. She checked the chamber and saw that it was loaded. The safety was on, so she put it into the waistband of her jeans, under her shirt, then grabbed the glass and poured some juice for ratboy. She took a step toward the door, then realized she was thirsty. She drank half, then poured some more for weaselface.

"Took you long enough," he said when she returned.

She saw that he'd eaten half the plate. Maybe he'd be in a better mood now. He slurped up the glass. "Get me more."

Marcia hurried back and got him another glass. She grabbed a handful of rice for herself and wolfed it down. She didn't know when she'd get to eat again. She needed to keep her strength up, now it wasn't just her life depending on her simpering performance.

"I'm waiting," he yelled out.

Nurul was done feeding Hana and stared at her with a scared expression as she hurried by on her way to Raymond. He grabbed the glass from her.

"Can I check out the old man?" Marcia asked tentatively.

"Let him die."

"You can't mean that." But as soon as the words were out of her mouth, Marcia realized they weren't true. Raymond meant it. He didn't care who he hurt or killed. She had to figure out an angle to get the old man some help. She *had* to.

Raymond continued to eat, staring at her with a satisfied gleam in his eye. "You're trying to figure me out, aren't you?"

She slowly nodded her head.

"I just don't register in your mind." His eyes twinkled. "I'm really a simple man. I eat. I shit. I fuck. Too bad you're not blonde and stacked, if you were, I'd be all over you. You're beginning to have the right attitude though, I'm kind of liking that."

Marcia shuddered. He said it so evenly like it was normal.

"Jesus, don't get your tit in a wringer. I told you, you're not my type. Just keep feeding me, and we'll be okay."

She couldn't help herself. "What will it hurt to help the old man?" she asked quietly.

"It's a waste of effort. A bullet is more expedient."

Marcia gnawed her bottom lip and gasped in pain. She'd forgotten her injury. "How long before we get to where we're going to?" she asked, changing the subject.

"I'd say we're almost there."

"Really?" Marcia spun around to see what he was looking at. Nothing made sense, all she could see was more jungle.

"It's almost dark, we're not going to be floating down the river in the middle of the night. Haven't you noticed all the turns we've had to navigate? Shit, Lesley, use your brain." He started to guide the boat toward the shore.

Oh no, Marcia saw the old man start to move. He was up on his hands and knees. What was he saying? She swung her head around and saw Raymond casually lifting his rifle.

CHAPTER FIVE

Zed heard a shot ring out as he saw the boat up ahead in the moonlight.

Was that a baby crying?

He ran for all that he was worth. Then he heard three more shots and splashing.

"Come on, Nurul, follow me," a woman yelled.

What the hell?

"I'm going to kill you, you bitch," a man's voice rang out. "Don't think this is the end of things. I'll find you."

Well, a man and a woman speaking English indicated that Raymond and Marcia were alive. Raymond sounded pissed, so score one for the good guys. Zed spotted two small shapes on the shore and as he got closer, the cries of the baby grew louder and louder.

"It's going to be okay, Nurul. I promise. Since you can't understand me, I also promise you that we'll find a unicorn that will take us to safety," Marcia said in a calm and comforting voice. Zed grinned. He liked her style. He wondered who the woman with the baby was. The other woman said something in a language Zed didn't understand, but he could tell she was crying along with the baby.

Zed was closer to the women than he was to the boat, but neutralizing Raymond was the smart move. He started toward the river, but then saw that Raymond was pushing off from the shore at the same time he lifted his rifle and fired more shots at the women.

"Get down," Zed shouted to Marcia. Zed raised his rifle and took aim at the same time Raymond dropped to the deck. He'd obviously heard Zed's shout. *Dammit.*

"Help us," Marcia shouted.

"I need to stop Raymond, or he'll come back for you," Zed objected.

"Forget Raymond. He hurt Hana, we need to get her to a doctor."

Zed looked back at the boat. Goddammit, it was already floating toward the middle of the river. He headed toward the women.

When he reached the trio, Marcia started talking again.

"Come on, we have to hurry. Raymond said there was some kind of camp down river."

Zed looked down at the little brunette giving him orders and barked out a laugh, he couldn't help it. "Before you start acting like my commanding officer, aren't you going to ask who I am?" Zed asked sardonically.

"You were shooting at Raymond and trying to help us. I pray to God you're one of the good guys."

Underneath all the dirt on her face, he saw the swelling on her cheek and eye, and he took note of the tear tracks. He couldn't tell if her attitude was an act or sheer bravado. He saw her lower lip tremble. Ah, hell.

"Marcia, didn't you know, the bad guys think they *are* the good guys," Zed said gently. He tried to get a look at the mother and baby, but the mother jerked away from him, cuddling her child close. "Who's Hana?" he asked Marcia.

"You called me Marcia," she said excitedly. "Mr. B. sent you." A smile broke over her face, and it hit him right in the gut. "Hana is the baby. He yanked her away from Nurul, I'm pretty sure he broke her arm, that's why she won't stop crying. After that, he threatened to kill Nurul's father if she didn't get Hana to stop crying." Marcia's voice broke, "Then the bastard killed him."

Zed watched as a tear spilled down her face.

"Marcia, we need to go," he said as he looked toward the water. Even though the boat was down river, he would still feel a lot better when they were hidden in the trees. "You can tell me everything when we're safer."

Marcia nodded.

"Are either you or Nurul injured, or can you walk?"

"We can walk," Marcia assured him.

When they got a little further in the jungle, then he could take a look at the little one's arm. If it was broken, he could work to set it. He could also call Dex to find out if any of the medication he had in his pack would be acceptable to give to a baby. He hoped so, he hated to hear her in so much pain.

"I'm going to lead, and we'll have Nurul follow me, and you'll take up the rear, okay?" he asked Marcia.

"Makes perfect sense," she said. "I'll holler if she's having trouble keeping up."

"Let me know if you're having trouble too. I can see he hit you," Zed said indicating her face. "What else did he do? Is there any immediate treatment that you need?"

"Seriously, I'm fine. We just need to take care of Hana and get the heck out of here."

He gave her a considering look and decided she wasn't lying to him. Using hand signals, Marcia and Zed made it clear to Nurul she needed to follow Zed into the jungle. He carefully chose the easiest path possible. When they had gone maybe a quarter of a mile and came to a log that would allow the women to rest against, Zed called a halt to their trek. Hana's shrieks had subsided to whimpers which were even more heart-wrenching. When he tried to help the mother sit down, she waved him off.

"You better let me," Marcia said.

Marcia helped to ease the young woman down onto the jungle floor, helping to hold the baby's head. When she was done, Marcia slumped down next to her, and Zed crouched down beside Marcia.

"Are you all right?" The bruising on her face had been agonizing to think about while they'd been walking. Zed kept his voice low, so he didn't disturb the baby.

"Yes, why?" Marcia asked.

"*Querida*, your face," Zed gently cupped her cheek. It felt inordinately warm to the touch, he prayed to God that none of the bones in her cheek had been broken.

"This is nothing," Marcia smiled grimly. "I've had worse when I played goalie on my soccer team. It's Hana we have to worry about."

"Fair enough," Zed kept his laugh quiet. "Tell me what happened," he said as he dropped his hand.

"I shot Raymond three times, but I failed. I didn't manage to kill him." Zed could tell that Marcia had been replaying the events in her mind and was angry at herself. She needed to calm down.

"Marcia, start at the beginning. Take me through what happened after Raymond kidnapped you. I especially want to know anything he might have said about why he took you, and what he planned to do with you."

Marcia didn't immediately start talking, she took a deep breath to collect her thoughts. She reminded him of one of his colleagues who was going to brief their lieutenant.

"After he took me, it was what you would expect. He tied me up, and it was a forced march to the river." Marcia looked off into space for a moment, and Zed knew there was more than she was telling him, but then she continued. "The important thing is, I finally figured out how to get information from him."

"How?"

"He likes women to be all subservient. As long as I kept up that attitude, I could ask him questions. He didn't tell me much, but he said some things. It was frustrating. When I tried to get more from him, he caught on and got angry."

Before he could ask her what, she was continuing.

"Did Mr. B. fill you in on the off-the-books ops he's been running?" she asked.

Zed nodded.

She took a deep breath and nodded. "Raymond was in on the one that went south, the one where the Saudi palace was bombed. His friends died, but he got out alive. He's holding a major grudge. At the heart of this, he wants Mr. B. to suffer, so torturing his daughters is high on his list, but the guy is greedy too."

Zed waited.

"There's somebody named Jefferies. I couldn't get a bead on who that was, but apparently, Raymond thinks Jefferies will pay for me. I don't know what my value is to him, or what he's going to do for me." She gave Zed a hard look, "I never let on that I wasn't Lesley Brockman."

"Good girl," he said soothingly.

Suddenly she wasn't in report mode. She raised her eyebrow. "I'm not a dog."

Zed bit his lip. "Well okay then," he drawled. "The phrase good girl has now been wiped from my vocabulary."

"Good boy." He raised an eyebrow, and she smirked.

"Okay, where was I? Oh yeah, Jefferies. He said he could get a really good price for me. He said something about Mr.

B. having access to a slush fund for his ops and being able to funnel money for my safe return. That's all I got before we got to the river…" She bit her lip.

She went silent, lost in thought.

"What happened?"

She shook her head.

"Marcia? How'd you get on the boat?"

She was still silent. Something had happened, but for some reason, she couldn't share it yet. Zed tried another tactic.

"How did you get a gun?"

"After we got on the boat, Raymond was demanding I make him food. Then he wanted something to drink, so I went into the galley. In one of the cupboards, I found a really old pistol. It was loaded, so I hid it in my jeans." She pulled it out of her pants and handed it to him.

"Jesus, Marcia, this is a relic. It could have gone off at any time and killed you."

She tried to pull it back out of his hand, but he wouldn't let go of it. "Hey, I wasn't stupid. I made sure the safety was on. Anyway, what the frick else was I supposed to do? Raymond was a murderer."

She was right. Zed took a deep breath. "I'm sorry."

She nodded her head. "Thanks." She peered up at him in the gloom of the night. "What's your name, anyway? Are you a Ranger?"

"Master Chief Petty Officer Dante Zaragoza at your service, Ma'am," Zed held out his hand.

He watched her frown for just a moment. Then her face cleared. "You're a SEAL." She took his hand, hers small and dainty in his.

"And you're smart. Most civilians don't know the different military ranks for the different branches of service."

"Yeah, well most people don't spend time in Harold Brockman's house. How's Mr. B., Debbie, and Christie? When Zed didn't immediately answer, she continued, "I know Mr. B. was bad this morning. Is your team going to be able to get him help in time?"

"Men are double-timing him out right now. They won't stop until he can be evacuated by helicopter. There is a surgeon waiting for him on the aircraft carrier. With this team taking care of him, he'll live," he assured her.

"Well okay then," she gave a sharp nod. "What can we do for Hana?" Zed was already shrugging out of his backpack.

"I'm going to make a call and verify what we can do for her." Zed looked over at the mother who was cradling her child and eying Zed warily. He gave her his warmest smile. She didn't respond in kind. He couldn't say he blamed her, considering her baby had just been injured by an American man. He grabbed the satellite phone out of his pack and called Dex.

"Have you tracked her down? Is she okay?" Dex immediately asked.

"Yes and yes," Zed answered. He saw Marcia's smile, it was obvious she could hear Dex.

"Thank God. Did you kill that son of a bitch?"

"Nope, but Marcia shot him."

"Is he dead?" Dex asked hopefully.

"Nope. I think the bullets might have hit his body armor, but I sure as hell don't want to get on her bad side."

Dex chuckled. Zed looked over at Marcia. Good. She was grinning. She'd been clear-headed and strong, but it was good to see her smiling.

"How are you planning on getting back?" Dex asked.

"First, I have a bit of a problem. It's a good one. Marcia managed to rescue a mother and child from that asshole, but not before he broke the kid's arm." Zed peered over at the child. "Dex, the kid is between one and two years old."

"Motherfucker!"

"My thought exactly. I hope to hell one of Marcia's three shots were in Raymond's balls."

Marcia snickered.

"Why isn't the kid screaming his head off?" Dex asked.

"She already has for the last forty-five minutes. She's down to just whimpering."

"How can I help?" Dex asked.

"You know the medication I have with me. Can you find out what is safe to administer to a kid who is…" again Zed looked at the toddler. "I'd say she is probably twenty to twenty-five pounds."

"Got it. Anything else?"

"Marcia, are you or the mother hurt?"

He watched her brown curls sway as she shook her head.

"Dex, Marcia and the mother are physically fine, except Marcia has a hell of a bruise on the side of her face. Can you get me the coordinates to the nearest outpost?"

"I'm on it. I'll call you back as soon as I have answers."

"Dex," Zed started.

"I'll make it fast."

"Good man," Zed said and disconnected.

"Zed, do you guys always read each other's minds?" Marcia asked.

Zed scrubbed his hand through his short black hair. "I think it's part of being a team." Hana started to cry again, and they both looked over at her. Marcia turned back to look at Zed. "Dex will call back in under three minutes, trust him." He liked the fact that even though he'd introduced himself as Dante, she'd picked up on the fact his name was Zed. She was smart.

Zed grinned as the phone in his hand vibrated.

"Whatchya got?" Zed asked.

"Normally, you would give the baby child strength Tylenol. What you're going to need to do, is give her one-third of a tablet of the Tylenol you have in your kit, then put her arm in a splint. In four hours, alternate with a third of a tablet of ibuprofen." Zed handed over his first-aid kit and flashlight to Marcia.

"Knife?" she held out her hand expectantly.

He shook his head. She rolled her eyes and handed him the tablet. He precisely shaved the dosage for the little girl and handed it to Marcia.

"Show-off," she said as she snagged his camelback water pack. "Do you have something for the baby to sip water out of?"

Zed fished around in his backpack and found his collapsible cup with his utensils and handed it to her. Marcia efficiently poured some water into the cup, and he watched as she showed the medicine to Nurul. She pantomimed feeding the pill to the baby, and the mother quickly caught on. With a little coaxing, Hana eventually swallowed the tablet along with some water.

"Zed, are you listening to me?" Dex asked.

"Yeah, yeah, I heard you," Zed interrupted. "You said the Eco-Tourist camp is about five miles down-river. I think that will take us about three hours to get there at night in this terrain. Tell me about it."

"It's tiny. It's run by a family. At the max, they have twelve tourists."

"How'd you find that out?"

"Their website," Dex laughed. "Okay, so three hours to get there?"

"Maybe four," Zed conceded.

Marcia gave him a pointed look.

"Hold on Dex. Marcia has something to say."

"Is there any way that we could rest here for an hour or so?" Marcia asked Zed.

Shit, he should have thought of that. She'd been on the move since they'd overtaken the camp that morning.

"Absolutely," he told her. Then he took a really good look at the mother and the baby. "It might be a good idea to just wait until morning before we start again."

Marcia gave him a relieved smile and turned to the others while he went back to talking to Dex.

"Did you hear that Dex?"

"I did. Zed, do you anticipate Raymond to be at the camp?"

He looked over at Marcia and saw she was occupied with getting the mom and baby comfortable for the night. He pulled out a survival blanket from his backpack and handed it to her and got up to walk a bit away, so he could have some privacy.

"You with me Zed?" Dex asked.

"Yeah, I'm here," Zed answered. "In answer to your question, yes, I think Raymond is going to be waiting for us. I don't have the full story yet, but he has a hard-on for Marcia. I'm not sure if he wants to kill her or capture her, but I can tell you this, he's not going to let her go."

"Then wait until the day after tomorrow for an extraction. That'll give Gray and the others time to be part of the rescue effort. They'll make sure you and Marcia are covered."

Zed looked over at the two women and the baby and weighed their options. He really wanted to get the child proper care. "I'll take it under advisement. We'll see how Hana is doing. I don't want her to suffer needlessly."

"Makes sense. Just keep me up-to-date."

"Dex, we have another issue I need you to check into. Marcia said that Raymond was planning on handing her over to a man named Jefferies. He said they expected Brockman would skim monies from the ops."

Dex was silent for a long moment. "Any amounts mentioned?"

"Nope."

"Okay. I'll check this out. This girl did good. She did damn good."

Zed looked over at Marcia and smiled slowly. "Yeah, she did," he agreed. "Call me when you find out something."

* * *

Zed walked over with a huge armful of leaves. "This should make it more comfortable for them to rest. I also have a change of clothes we can lay out on top of this to act as a sheet." Marcia watched in fascination as Zed made a makeshift bed in less than two minutes. Nurul gave him a sad smile and nodded her head in thanks.

"Looks like Hana is feeling better," he said.

Zed's teeth shone white in the dark. The man had an outstanding smile.

"I think the medicine and splint are allowing her to sleep. I just hope that Nurul will be able to sleep tonight." Marcia shoved the heel of her hand against her forehead. She couldn't get the picture of Raymond shooting Nurul's father out of her mind. She jumped when Zed's hand touched her shoulder.

"Are you going to be okay, Marcia?"

"Oh yeah, sure. Why wouldn't I be? I'm the bait who managed to get Nurul and her father to come to the shore and allowed that monster come into their lives, why wouldn't I be okay?" The pain in her cheek increased tenfold as she ground her teeth together, trying to stop a sob from escaping.

"Marcia, you can't blame yourself."

"Oh really?" she said bitterly. "Who else is there to blame? I should have refused Raymond. I should have fought him. I should have just told him no."

"You had no way of knowing this is what would have happened," Zed said softly. She wanted to shrug off his hand, it felt warm and comforting, and she didn't deserve it. She ground her teeth together even harder, then gasped at the pain that pierced up into her eye. Zed cupped both of her shoulders.

"Querida, you have to relax, you're hurting yourself."

"I deserve to hurt," she cried out.

Nurul called out her name. Dammit. Marcia brushed off Zed's hands and bent to Nurul who had been resting with Hana.

"Shhhhh, I'm fine Nurul," Marcia crooned. "Everything's fine," she smiled. She stroked her hand down Nurul's arm. "Go to sleep. Everything will be just fine, I promise," Marcia continued to speak softly until the young woman's eyes closed.

"You're good at that."

Marcia turned tiredly to look at Zed. "I'm good at what?" she asked.

"Giving comfort."

"Yeah…well…" What could she say to that?

Nurul moved, it was clear she had fallen asleep and was now stretching out. Marcia scooted away from her to give her a little more space, but that meant she moved closer to Zed.

"I ran out of blankets and extra clothes," he said.

"I don't need it. I can just lay on the ground."

Zed gave her a considering look. "That is definitely an option. I can go and get you more leaves, and I'll try to make you something as comfortable as possible. Or you can just lean on me. It's your choice."

Well, that wasn't a choice at all. The man was huge. After spending a day with another big man who was a psychopath Marcia was stunned at the level of trust she had for Zed. It was as if a long-buried part of her recognized his innate honor.

"I don't know. The cold ground or your body heat. I have one question. Do you snore?"

Zed chuckled, and Marcia grinned. He slowly reached out and put his arm around her shoulders, bringing her closer to his side.

"Kane is the one who snores, we're constantly rolling him over during missions. Since nobody has kicked me, I figure you're safe."

The man's smile was positively wicked. Marcia took one last look at Nurul and Hana, then relaxed against Zed's warmth.

"So how often do you SEALs cuddle for body heat?"

"Every mission," he quickly replied. "I spoon with Cullen, he's our medic."

Marcia giggled. As soon as she heard the laughter come out of her mouth, she slapped her hand over her face. How could she laugh after what she'd done?

"Honey, what is it?" Zed turned her, so that they were face to face.

"What am I thinking?" she gulped. "How can I possibly smile at anything after what I've done?"

"Marcia, you've done nothing wrong," Zed said softly.

She tried to jerk out of his hold, but he was having none of it.

"Let me go," she hissed.

"No."

"You've got to," she let out a little sob. "You've got to. Don't be nice to me."

"Oh Baby, why wouldn't I be nice to you?"

Marcia tried to get up, but he held her even closer to his body.

"Honey, listen to me, what you're feeling is normal. You've been through so much today. You need to rest."

"You've got to let me go," she whimpered. "I need to be alone."

"That's the last thing you need," he said softly. "Marcia, you had no way of knowing what was going to happen, now did you?"

She didn't answer. She felt his big hand cupping the back of her head, his other hand was stroking her back. She shoved her face into his chest, heedless of the slight pain in her cheek because the comfort she received more than made up for it.

"He killed him like he was nothing. Oh God, Zed, it was awful. Nurul lost everything, her home and her father, all because of me."

Zed was saying something, she couldn't hear him over her sobs, but she could feel him, feel his warmth, feel his strength. Marcia had no idea how long she stayed like that, but when she came back to herself, she found herself on his lap, whimpering. He was holding her as tenderly as Nurul had held Hana.

Why didn't she feel embarrassed? She pushed away just enough so she could look at his face and saw compassion and empathy. It was magical. Another tear dripped down her face, and he caught it with his thumb.

"You didn't tell me not to cry," she said in wonder.

"Why would I?"

"Because…because…"

"Oh, honey," he pulled her close again, and she rested her head against his chest, soaking in his comfort like a flower soaks in the sun. She felt him shift. He handed her the cup filled with water.

"You need to drink," he said quietly. Her mind went back to when she'd said the same thing to Christie, and she nodded. She took the cup and sipped the warm water.

"What about you?"

"I've had some."

Now that the mundane had entered the quiet of the jungle, Marcia realized the intimacy of her position. She shifted, pushing to get off his lap. Zed didn't question. With easy strength, he moved her, so she was once again resting by his side.

"Better?" he asked.

She nodded shyly.

"Morning's going to come sooner than you think. We're going to need to get a move on."

"Why? I thought we were going to wait until tomorrow night before the helicopter was going to come and rescue us."

"I want to get close to the camp, then I'm going to acquire food. Hana especially needs milk."

How could she not have considered that? She pushed the heel of her hand into her forehead, so angry with herself.

"You need to stop that," Zed said as he pulled her hand away.

"I should have thought of that. It's my job to think of things. I'm supposed to be taking care of them."

"Why?" he gave her a questioning look. "Why is it your job?"

"What do you mean why?"

"Marcia, you're twenty-three. You just met Nurul today. Why is it your job to be taking care of her and her baby?"

"It's always my job to take care of people," she said reasonably. "It's what I do."

His brown eyes glittered down at her. He was so handsome with his black hair and sharp cheekbones. "What did you ask?"

"I asked who do you take care of?"

"Mr. B., the girls, Lesley...Rick" Why was he asking these questions? Why was he frowning?

"Who takes care of you?"

"Mrs. B. was wonderful." God, she hated thinking of her. It hurt worse when she died than when her parents did. And then a month later Rick said he was sick of how moody she'd become. He said she wasn't paying enough attention to him. She tried, she really tried, but Debbie and Christie needed her, and she was still so sad about Mrs. B.'s death, she just couldn't give him the attention he wanted.

"She died, didn't she?" Zed asked.

"Yeah," Marcia nodded. "Then everything fell apart."

He stroked her shoulder. "Can you tell me?"

It must have been the quiet of the jungle, the warm air, the intimacy of the silky night that had her considering talking to this man. But she'd bared so much of her soul, she needed more.

"Have you ever experienced loss Zed?" she finally asked.

"I'm thirty-six, in the military, so yeah," he breathed out heavily, "people who have meant a lot to me have died."

She could see the truth in his eyes. "Just your teammates?"

"No," he said quietly. "My *abuela* right after I became a SEAL."

"It's killing me Christie and Debbie have been subjected to it."

"They'll survive, they have their father."

"And me."

"Why? Why do you think you have to take care of everyone?"

It was the first time that anyone had ever asked her that question, and Marcia didn't know how to answer it. She looked up at him, confused.

"Come closer. It's time for you to get some sleep," Zed said as he tugged her closer to his side. With one last look over at Nurul and Hana, Marcia settled in against Zed and closed her eyes.

CHAPTER SIX

He was sick of this shit. All he wanted to do was take out Raymond, but he couldn't take the time to search for him. He needed to focus on getting food for the women and especially milk for Hana.

Zed saw the houseboat tied up with two canoes and one twelve seat motorboat. It was an hour before dawn, the camp was quiet, but just in case he was spotted, he dressed in the civilian clothes Wyatt had obtained for him. He had body armor, a pistol, and two knives hidden underneath his clothes. He didn't bring his rifle with him, he'd left it with Marcia.

He sure as fuck didn't intend to be spotted, but the rule was to plan for the worst, and hope for the best. There was one building that looked more lived in, Zed assumed it was where the owners lived. The three cabins with thatched roofs were identical, down to the pots of flowers on the porch.

Zed saw a light in the owner's house, then the front door opened. A woman came out. He slipped behind one of the cabins, watching as she walked to the side of the house. In the quiet of the morning, her voice carried.

"Good morning. I hope you didn't mind staying in our old cabin."

"Alice, it was a lot more comfortable than the houseboat. I really appreciate it. I just want to thank you for fitting me in for the tour at the last minute."

"Mr. Raymond, it is our pleasure," the small woman said in accented English. "I came to tell you that there is a call for you on the satellite phone inside. I think it is the one you're waiting for."

"That's good news," Raymond sounded positively gleeful. They both came into view and Zed finally had his first look at Raymond. The man was big and blonde and was totally aware of his environment. Zed had his gun in his hand before he even realized it, but then Raymond had positioned the woman so he was always between her and the small house. He was a cautious bastard.

"After your call, you can have an early breakfast. Usually, the tourists get up an hour or two after sunrise, and I make breakfast in the common area." She ushered him into the house.

Zed considered his options. Attempting to take out Raymond now should be pretty damned easy even if he was cautious, but if he failed, he'd be leaving Marcia, Nurul, and the baby defenseless. Her having the rifle for protection really didn't mean a damn thing. But if he waited until the team came, then Raymond would be toast, and Marcia would be one hundred percent safe.

Get the milk. Get the food.

He hated being thirty-six. Wisdom sucked. There is no way he would have made this decision in his twenties. He headed toward the common area to get the milk and food.

Zed's lip tilted upward when he saw the small area in the middle of the camp that had open seating and a thatched roof. The good news was there were three dilapidated large coolers. All three of them had padlocks, apparently, the couple who owned the camp didn't trust their guests, and he wasn't going to do anything to instill trust.

Zed continued to watch around the area, listening for anything that indicated he wasn't alone. When he was sure he was alone, he got out his K-Bar and broke the lock on the largest cooler.

Paydirt!

Riceballs, biscuits, bananas, shrimp, sliced cucumbers, bottles of water, and three pitchers of liquid, one of which was milk. Quickly, he poured out one of the liter bottles of water and filled it with the milk. He filled the empty duffle bag he'd brought with him with his loot and took another look around as he quietly closed the lid of the cooler.

He would need to hide the women deeper in the jungle after his raid on the food, just to be on the safe side. He left the camp the opposite way he came in, so he wouldn't have to go past the couple's home. He didn't want any chance of running into Raymond.

* * *

Blood. There was blood everywhere. How could there be so much blood?

Marcia stumbled. Her leg hurt so bad. She fell down, and spears of sunlight were piercing her eyes. She slammed them shut.

What the heck was wrong with her? She couldn't sit up.

"Marcia?" Nurul's voice was coming from far away. Marcia opened her eyes and could only see a black shadow she had to assume was Nurul. Finally, her beautiful brown features came into focus, then they were at the end of a long tunnel.

Did she hear a baby crying?

Get it together Price.

"Marcia?" Nurul patted her face, then pulled on her arm. Marcia tried to sit up, pushing up with her arms and legs and let out a shriek. Her leg felt on fire. She looked down, it was covered in blood. And there was still portions of flesh that weren't hers attached. Then she remembered. The snake.

She looked over at the huge snake that had slithered down out of the tree. It had been headed toward Hana, and Marcia had pushed them out of the way. Then the python had sunk its teeth into her leg then began wrapping its coils around her and started to squeeze. And squeeze. And squeeze.

She still didn't know how she had managed to pull the rifle over to her and pull the trigger. But she had. She'd shot over and over again. Then there was nothing, everything went dark.

Nurul stopped trying to pull her up, instead, she was doing something that hurt.

"Stop. Please stop," Marcia whimpered. She propped herself up and saw the young woman straining to pry open the jaws of the dead snake. It was the last part of the reptile that was attached to Marcia. As soon as Nurul got it off, she threw it into the trees.

Nurul then started murmuring to her in the same tone she used when she had tried to calm baby Hana. Marcia moaned as Nurul started to roll up her pant leg. At the top of her ankle, she could see the bite marks of the snake. At least it wasn't poisonous. Now how in the heck did she know that?

God her head hurt. She lowered herself back down on the ground and rolled her head sideways, so she wasn't looking up into the sun. Oh yeah, Christie's report on reptiles. Pythons and Boa Constrictors, not poisonous, just liked to hug you to death. Lucky her.

"Marcia?"

Shit, she'd passed out again. Marcia winced. Her head hurt, her leg hurt, and she was now saying swear words in her head. Life was just getting better and better. Well, at least it was Nurul talking and not Raymond.

Nurul was stroking her face. She was also holding Hana who was crying softly. She was really hot. Really, really hot. It seemed Nurul knew what the problem was because she was holding the straw from Zed's camelback to Marcia's lips.

Marcia shook her head and pointed to Hana.

Nurul shoved the straw back at Marcia. The woman was determined, Hana must have had her water Marcia thought, so she drank.

She dropped her head back into the dirt and winced. When she opened her eyes again, Nurul's face wavered, and for just a second, she thought she was in a sunny kitchen in Virginia.

"Mrs. B?" Marcia asked. "Mrs. B? I thought you were dead." She tried to reach out and touch the woman she loved like a mother.

"Marcia, what in the hell happened?"

Mrs. B.'s calm blue eyes morphed into fierce black eyes.

"Who are you?" Marcia asked.

* * *

Nurul scrabbled away from Marcia and started running off into the jungle. What in the hell? She was leaving him with her baby?

"Nurul?" Zed shouted after the small, young woman.

Well obviously, she was healthy if she could run that well, and he'd already checked out Hana, and except for the screaming, there was no blood on her. Nope, Marcia was the injured person. When Zed had heard the shots, he had raced to get to the women. To find Marcia lying on the jungle floor covered in blood and gore was even scarier.

"Marcia, can you talk to me? Can you tell me what happened?"

"What? What's going on?" she asked, clearly in a daze.

"Marcia, why did you shoot the rifle?" he pointed to the SCAR lying on the ground a few feet away from her.

"I don't know."

Her golden-brown eyes stared up at him, pleading. She swallowed heavily, then gasped. Zed saw her stomach undulate and knew what was coming next. With gentle hands, he put his arm under her back and his hand beneath her head, so he could turn her. She hissed, then Marcia started to heave, the contents of her stomach decorating the floor of the jungle.

Nurul shouted at him. He looked up and saw the remains of a python head in her hands. She knelt down and struggled to pull up the hem of Marcia's jean leg.

"No, it hurts," Marcia gasped, then started to gag.

Zed now understood what had happened, except for who had shot the python. He waved Nurul away, and the woman went to pick up her daughter. Marcia started to move in his arms. He tried to keep her calm.

"Shhhh. It's okay."

She pushed at him.

"I've got you," he assured her.

"Let me move," she said clearly. "I want to get my nose away from the aroma of vomit and dirt, otherwise I'll never stop throwing up."

"We don't want that, now do we?" He gently moved her away from the puddle.

"No, we really don't want me upchucking again." She took some deep breaths. "Look, I'm fine now."

"Just stay still." He brushed her sweat-drenched hair from her forehead and watched her drag in more air.

"Did you get everything? Milk for Hana?"

Zed chuckled. He guessed she was doing better if she could remember what he had been out looking for. Out of the corner of his eye, he saw Nurul investigating the contents of the duffle bag.

"Yes ma'am, I carried out my mission successfully." He felt her relax. "Now, would you mind telling me what in the fucking hell happened here?" he asked in a calm and relaxed voice.

He saw her swallow once, then twice. "Come on, take pity."

He took a deep breath, so he didn't come unglued. This whole set-up had him shaken, and it shouldn't. It was his job to be able to handle any situation but seeing her so damn helpless was killing him.

"Goddammit, I am taking pity," he bit out.

Zed saw her eyes fill up with tears. Ahhh damn. "Marcia, it's okay. You survived. You did great. Everything's going to be fine, honey." He tried to pull her in closer, but she shook her head.

"Why are you yelling at me?" she asked in a dejected voice.

"I didn't yell," he said, surprised.

"You swore. You said 'goddammit.' That's the same as yelling. I can't handle it right now, okay?" How could she sound defiant with tears in her voice?

"I'm sorry." He meant it too.

Her eyes searched his, then she nodded.

Nurul peered over Zed's shoulder. She shoved a liter bottle of milk toward her. She kept repeating a word over and over. Finally, she pretended to drink from the bottle, and Marcia realized Nurul wanted her to drink some milk.

"She's right. You need to eat and drink," Zed said.

"I'll just throw up again."

Zed stood up with her in his arms, and Marcia let out a surprised squeak.

"Just how strong are you?"

"Strong enough," he said as he settled her against the log, well away from the gore of the dead snake. What he wouldn't give for some 7-Up and tapioca pudding, right about now, he just knew that would settle her stomach. Instead, he pulled out a wadded-up ball of rice and a warm bottle of water and squatted down next to Marcia. "Wanna rinse out your mouth?"

She greedily lunged at the water bottle. He watched as she swished and spit, then she took long sips of the water.

"Don't overdo, otherwise, you'll be right back to square one," he warned.

"Huh?"

"Marcia, your stomach's going to protest too much water too soon. Take little sips." He eased the water bottle out of her hands, then gave her the plastic wrapped ball of rice. "How about a bite of this?"

Marcia pinched off a little of the white sticky rice and savored it, then swallowed and smiled.

"Good?" he asked.

"Yes," she said as she took a bigger piece.

"Why don't you concentrate on eating while I take a look at your leg. Then you can kindly tell me about your adventures with a snake," he smiled.

She gave him a half-hearted smile, but at least she wasn't close to tears this time. She stretched her neck, then slowly closed her eyes.

"I think it was a python," she started.

Zed continued to listen to her as he started to examine her leg. Everything above the knee looked okay, but below the knee, they had a fuck-load of a problem. Her canvass shoe was having trouble containing the swelling and so was her pant leg. Around her ankle, where there was nothing to contain it, it was swollen to three times its normal size. He had to bandage it ASAP.

"Repeat that," Zed said to Marcia. He'd been listening with half an ear, and now he needed to make sure he'd heard her correctly.

"I said pythons aren't poisonous," she answered him.

That's exactly what he remembered, but he'd wanted Dex to confirm it for him. Hearing her tell him the same thing he remembered made him feel much better. But even if the snake didn't have venom, all the bacteria needed to be cleaned out of her wound. He grabbed some disinfectant pads out of his pack, pulled out his knife and a roll of bandages.

He cut through her jeans just a little, so he could get to the bite.

"Son of a motherless goat!"

He looked up at her, and she gave him a haughty wave. "Just keep going," she gritted out.

What the hell was she going to say when he applied the alcohol wipe?

"Fudge Nugget!" He could hear both tears and laughter in her voice.

"Almost done." Nurul was stroking her hair. Zed quickly applied a tight bandage around her lower leg and ankle. This time she didn't say anything entertaining, she just gasped with the pain.

He checked his watch. Dex had said the helo was due to arrive between six and eight tonight. That was worthy of more than just the phrase Fudge Nugget.

Now that her leg had been tended to, he needed to figure out why she'd been so disoriented. "Marcia, I need to look at the back of your head, I think you hit it."

"Huh?"

"When I got here, you weren't lucid. You hissed when I touched your scalp."

Zed got closer to her and tilted her chin up so he could look into her eyes. Thank God her pupils looked good. She turned her neck, and he felt a goose-sized egg on the back of her head.

Shit!

"Yeah, you've got a hell of a bump back here."

"I remember now," her eyes brightened, "it was when I took the shot at the snake. I leaned back as far as I could, so I was shooting at the end of it, and the rifle plowed into my shoulder. I ended up hitting my head against the log. But I killed the son of a bitch." She slammed her hand over her mouth.

"Yes. Yes, you did," Zed grinned. "You got the fudge nugget. I think being kidnapped twice, being forced marched through a jungle, and almost killed by a python allows you to swear like a sailor."

"It's just one of the few things I've had control over, you know?"

He did understand that. He understood it all too well.

"Querida, let's put this one down to a head injury, shall we?"

He watched her consider it, then finally nod.

Nurul had been watching the two of them closely as she alternated feeding her baby milk and banana. When Zed pointed to the blanket, she immediately got it so Marcia could use it as a pillow. Then she sat down next to her and gave Zed a worried look. He gave her his best smile, but she didn't seem to be buying it. He pulled the satellite phone out of his backpack and contacted Dex.

"Did you get the food?"

Zed paced away from the women as he began answering. "Food situation has been taken care of. Goddamn python bit Marcia and coiled around her leg. She shot it, but her right leg underneath the knee is swollen to twice its normal size. It'd be three times if it weren't for her shoe and jeans."

"Dammit."

"There's more. She's got a bad concussion. She wasn't lucid when I arrived, and she's vomited. Her pupils are good. But we need her out of here, three minutes ago. We can't wait for the team."

"Got it. I'll get back to you as soon as there's a plan."

"Thanks."

CHAPTER SEVEN

How come trying not to throw up, only made her think of vomit? She should never have eaten part of that banana. Did he have to step in every hole and climb over every log? Couldn't Zed find a flat trail?

Marcia gritted her teeth and breathed through her nose trying to force down the nausea, but the more she bit down, the more her head hurt.

"We're going to be there soon," he said.

How come he didn't sound out of breath?

"Marcia? Are you with me?"

"Don't want to talk," she gritted out. "I'm about ready to blow chunks."

"Should we stop?" Zed asked as he slowed down.

She shook her head. Darn it, that was a mistake. She groaned. He stopped.

As soon as she was on the ground, she rolled over and puked. When she was done, she saw the water bottle under her face. She grabbed it and rinsed out her mouth.

"Let's go," she muttered.

"Nurul needs a moment," Zed said.

She looked around and realized Zed was holding Hana. Marcia blinked slowly, trying to bring them into focus. He was stroking the baby's head, his lean fingers so gentle against the child's soft skin. He bent and kissed her forehead. He must have felt her gaze on him because he looked up and smiled.

"Do you have children?" Marcia asked.

"No."

"Nieces? Nephews?"

He got a funny look on his face, then finally answered. "Probably soon."

Before she had a chance to probe further, Nurul returned. "We should get going," Marcia said.

"Are you sure?"

"When is the helicopter due?" she asked.

Zed looked down at his watch. "Soon."

She gave him a pointed glance.

"Less than an hour."

"So, we need to go."

"Yes," he said as he stood up and handed Hana to her mother. Marcia held out her arms, and Zed lifted her up. He waited while Nurul adjusted Hana into a comfortable position. Marcia vaguely remembered Zed cutting up some medicine, and Nurul coaxing her daughter to take it. She couldn't wait until the little girl could have proper care. Then Zed started walking and once again all she could concentrate on was focusing on the landscape ahead of her, so she wouldn't get dizzy.

After a few minutes went by, Zed started talking. "I need to fill you in on the plan."

"When did you make a plan?"

"You were out of it, one of the times we stopped to rest. We've got four good men coming in on the helicopter. I don't know them, but the captain vouches for them."

"Will they be able to land?"

"Yeah, there's space."

"What about Raymond?"

"Once he hears the helicopter, he's going to know you're being rescued. He's also going to know we're going to want to take him out. He'll know he's outmanned, so we think he's going to make a run for it."

Marcia's fingers tightened on Zed's jacket. She hoped so. Marcia didn't want anyone else to get injured because of her. She shut her eyes, thinking of Nurul's father. Even now, she could hear the thud his body made as it bounced off the deck from the strike of the bullet. Her eyes opened when she heard Hana start to cry.

"Zed?"

"It's okay, we're almost there now."

"Alice," Nurul said. Zed stopped and turned to look at Nurul, the young woman was pointing through the thinning trees. "Alice," she smiled, excited. "Ahmed," she was grinning now.

"I'll be damned. I should have guessed it. She knows the people who run the camp," Zed said.

"How do you know them?" Marcia asked as she shifted in his arms. Everything hurt and trying to get comfortable was almost impossible.

"I overheard Raymond speaking to the woman who was running the camp." Zed knelt down on one knee and set Marcia down. "I need to call Dex and find out the ETA." As soon as he said that, the faint sound of a helicopter could be heard in the distance.

"Guess you don't need to call him," Marcia said. He gathered her back up into his arms and nodded for Nurul to follow him. He went quicker as the trees thinned out. The helicopter sounds were much clearer, but the sound was upsetting Hana and she was crying even more loudly. None of the sounds were good for Marcia's headache, but that wasn't really relevant, now was it? Power through. She just needed to power through.

"They're really early," she heard Zed mutter as he jogged to the edge of the clearing. Marcia saw the camp, and everyone was clustered, looking up at the helicopter. It was still tough for her to make out the markings, but it looked kind of big. No wonder people were looking at it, it was going to cause damage to some of the cabins with the wind from the blades.

"Alice," Nurul yelled out. She tried to push ahead of Zed, but he moved in front of her, blocking her way.

"No," he thundered at the young mother. Marcia looked up at him in confusion. Hana stopped crying for a moment when confronted with Zed's loud yell. "Nobody move."

"Zed, what's wrong?"

"It's not one of ours."

He dropped down to his knees and set Marcia down at the same time he pulled Nurul down beside Marcia. "Marcia, I need you to keep Nurul here while I check things out."

"Are you sure? How can you tell?" Marcia asked.

"You've got to stay here and out of sight. Keep Nurul with you," he shouted as he took off at a run. He had his rifle in his hand. It took everything she had not to call out after him. He was a SEAL, but still, he was the man who'd just kissed a baby. Please God, please God, please God, keep him safe. Marcia blinked her eyes. Where had he gone? How could he have just disappeared?

* * *

The helicopter should have been a Seahawk, instead, it was a Russian Mi-17, Zed could tell because of the tail rotor mounting and the lack of double doors. He knew the Mi's came cheap and people like the Thorne Group, and whoever these mercs were, used them. Raymond must have called in for backup.

Fuck!

Good news was he didn't see that it had been beefed up with external cannon, machine guns, anti-tank guarded missiles, or rocket pods. Of course, who was to say what kind of firepower it had inside or how many armed men.

Zed saw a climbable tree up ahead. He wasted no time shimmying up and getting into position. He had his gun rifle mounted between two branches and his satellite phone out in seconds. Before Dex could even talk, he started.

"Got an enemy helo landing. Inform incoming helicopter."

"Describe it."

"Russian Mi-17. No ordnance on the outside. What's the ETA on the—"

"Less than twenty minutes."

"Give them a heads up. Gotta shoot some fish in a barrel." Zed disconnected as the single side door opened and the first man exited. Where was Raymond? Zed peered through the scope on his rifle. Five men in total exited the helicopter, still no sign of Raymond to greet them. Peering into the dark interior of the helo, it didn't look like there was anybody else in there but the pilot. He could see a mounted machine gun, but it wasn't manned.

"You have to be kidding me," Zed muttered. Raymond came out of the house flanked by Alice and a man who must be her husband. There wasn't a shot. Two of the armed men from the helicopter came over to Raymond. Zed waited. They managed to position themselves right in front of the two natives and Zed's ultimate target.

"Enough of this noise." Zed hoped when he took out the two men he could, it would make Raymond move, and he could get to him. He peered through his scope, blocked out all the noise of the jungle. Taking one breath in and expelling it, he took one shot, then in a fraction of a second, he moved the rifle minutely and took the second man. Two dead. Raymond had hit the ground, pulling Alice on top of him.

Crack!

Crack!

Zed ducked as a branch hit his back. He slithered down part of the tree, then jumped out, knowing his hiding spot had been discovered.

Crack!

Zed ducked again. The tree trunk was hit. Shit, that was close. He made sure to keep it between him and the clearing as he took off at a run, then he zoomed to the left, behind another tree. He looked behind and could see someone coming toward him. He needed to take a shot, he didn't need them coming into the jungle, he needed to go at them. He needed to keep them away from the women.

Zed positioned himself behind another tree and took aim. He watched as he hit the man in the neck. Perfect. He plowed forward, but unfortunately, from his point of view on the ground, he couldn't see where anybody else was in the clearing. He needed to get closer.

Zed moved to the point where he could peer into the clearing. He saw Raymond, once again near the house, his arm around Alice's neck, was using her as a shield.

A woman's scream, then a man's scream came from one of the cabins. What the hell?

"Give me Lesley!" Raymond yelled.

Zed's head swiveled back to see that Raymond was now in the common area, his back up against a pole, still using Alice as a shield as he fired high-velocity rounds into the guest cabin closest to him. That's why there were screams coming from inside.

"I know you're out there, give me Lesley."

"You're in no position to negotiate," Zed yelled back.

"I'm willing to kill everybody in this fucking place. Rogers, kill the civilians," Raymond shouted. Zed saw the tip of the rifle that had been peeking out from behind the cabin disappear. He watched helplessly as bullet holes pelted the opposite cabins and more shrieks were heard from inside that one. The door flew open, and a woman ran out.

"Go back inside," Zed yelled, then watched in horror as a plume of blood burst on her back and she flew down the stairs. She didn't move.

"Give me Lesley, or they all die," Raymond's voice rang out across the clearing.

"I'm here," Marcia's voice could be heard faintly behind him.

Raymond laughed.

It wasn't over. Someone still needed to show themselves to get Marcia, and when they did, Zed would kill them, it was that simple.

"I want you too," Raymond yelled. "Bring her to me."

"I don't think so," Zed replied.

Another volley of shots went into the cabin, and another woman's cries were heard.

"It's like shooting fish in a barrel. This is fun, isn't it Rogers?"

"Damn right it's fun," a man called back to Raymond, his Southern accent thick and out of place here in the Borneo jungle.

Zed closed his eyes. He prayed for the Navy copter, but there was still no sign of it. Maybe by the time he got Marcia?

"You have five minutes, then Rogers and Larks start shooting up all three cabins. Alice told me she has a full house this weekend. What is that Alice?"

Zed watched as Raymond shook the woman. He couldn't hear what she said.

"Eleven. Two of them are children. I bet some of them are injured right now. What do you want to bet?"

Where was that damn helicopter?

"You have five minutes."

"She's injured, I have to carry her."

"Five minutes," Raymond said carelessly. "Come on, you're a SEAL, aren't you? I could do it. The clock starts now."

Where was the fifth man? Zed pulled out his satellite phone and ran. "Where's the fucking helicopter?" he panted.

"Talk to me," Dex said patiently.

"Got three bad guys. At least twelve live civilians they are threatening to kill. They've killed one if not more," Zed thought of the shots that had blown holes into the cabin.

"I can't understand you," Dex said.

"What?"

"Stop running and talk."

"Where's the helo?"

"Ten minutes out."

Zed stopped talking and just ran for all he was worth.

"Zed? Zed? Zed? Talk to me," he heard Dex continuing to call out to him, but he didn't put the phone up to his ear. Goddammit, why couldn't he be helmeted with his com working? He hated not having his equipment.

He stopped short when he came upon Marcia, Nurul, and the baby. Nurul stood up. He put his hand in the air and shook his head. He motioned for her to sit back down. It was clear she was frightened out of her mind. She had to have heard the gunfire and the yelling. She hesitated, so Zed pressed her shoulders to force her back down to the ground. He again made the motion for her to stay put.

Marcia placed her hands together in prayer. "Nurul, please," she begged. Then Marcia too, pressed her hands down on Nurul's shoulders, indicating Nurul should stay seated. Nurul nodded her head in agreement, and Marcia gave a smile of relief.

"Zed, answer me," Dex's voice could be heard on the phone.

"Here, talk to Dex while I carry you," Zed said as he tossed her the phone and picked her up.

"I can walk."

"Sure, you can," he said sarcastically. He picked her up, then shifted her in his arms and started jogging toward the clearing. "Why the fuck did you call out? I ought to blister your ass for that stunt."

Zed kept his focus on the terrain ahead and giving Marcia shit, blocking out the horror of the woman dying and the possible deaths of children back at the camp. Then he heard Dex's voice.

"Talk to Dex, tell him the Navy helicopter needs to come in hot." He leaped over a fallen log, then avoided a hole. He listened as best he could to the conversation.

"They were shooting, people died. Zed's going to hand me over."

There was a pause, he couldn't hear Dex's response.

"He is, I'm not lying. There is no other plan."

"Wait, we're stopping."

Zed knelt down and pulled out his two guns. His rifle was still positioned behind his back as he held Marcia. "Take the gun and hold up the phone." He got back up, holding the other gun under her shirt as he carried her.

"Dex," Zed started talking. "The plan is to stall until they hear the Navy chopper. As soon as they do, I'm falling on top of Marcia, and taking out who I can. Hopefully, we have a sniper in the helicopter who can take out a bogey or two."

"Negative. I've checked," Dex said.

"Then have them lay down fire where they can. I want confusion. They need to avoid the cabins, that's where the civilians are, just to hit the ground in the compound. Got it? If they can't be spot-on accurate, I don't want them trying for the bad-guys because one of them is using a civilian as a shield."

"Got it. Keep this line open. I need to know what's going on to feed the Seahawk."

"How?" Marcia asked.

"I'm using radio communication with them," Dex explained.

"Go silent," Zed commanded. "Marcia, hide the phone." Zed saw her shove it down the front of her pants, then cover it with her shirt. She had the pistol in her hand. "Shield the pistol," he directed her. She shoved that up under her shirt as well.

They broke through the tree line.

"Just in time," Raymond crowed loudly. "We're all going to the helicopter."

"Let Alice go," Zed said.

"You have no leverage," Raymond laughed as the man named Rogers came out from behind the cabin with his rifle cradled in his arm.

Whap. Whap.

"What the fuck?" Raymond cried as he looked up. A Seahawk helicopter was clearly visible. Still too far away to lay down fire. Zed pretended to trip. He went down on both knees.

"Get up, you useless piece of shit."

Marcia went limp and rolled onto the ground. What a good little actress.

"What's wrong with her?"

"What isn't wrong with her?" Zed shot back. He pretended to scoop her up and slipped again.

"Quit fucking playing around!"

Zed stood up with Marcia in his arms. Dirt flew up as he heard the gunshots from the helicopter. Screams came from every cabin and from Alice. Marcia lay limp in his arms, he looked down for just a second to make sure she wasn't really unconscious and saw a small smile playing on her mouth.

"I'm going to kill her. Blow her head away. I'm going to enjoy it too, if you don't move your ass and put Lesley into the helicopter, right fucking now." Zed looked up and saw Raymond moving backward, dragging Alice by the neck to the helicopter. Rogers had his rifle trained on him and Marcia. He finally saw the fifth guy come out from behind Alice's house, he had a small man by the hair who must have been Ahmed, Alice's husband.

"Move it SEAL-boy, get Lesley onto the helicopter, she's our payday."

"I'll get us to the helicopter," Zed said loudly. He needed to get information to Dex. "Just don't let your other two men shoot any more of the civilians."

More shots from the Navy helicopter fired into the ground. Rogers lifted his gun and shot into the middle cabin, he shot low where there was more of a chance of a kill shot.

"Get her onto our helicopter now, or the next bullets go into the host and hostess."

The rotors of the Mi Helicopter started up, and it mixed with the wind of the Seahawk helicopter as it came down really low. Rogers who didn't have a hostage was shot in the head by someone in the Seahawk.

Yay for their side.

Alice and Ahmed were both being dragged back toward the helicopter. A rope dropped down from the Seahawk. Zed saw the man holding Ahmed move his gun away from the man's head and point to the man rappelling from the helicopter, and Zed dropped Marcia, falling on top of her as he shot the bogey before the bad guy could get off a shot.

"Bastard," Raymond yelled.

Zed jolted as he felt a bullet slam into his neck.

Please, God, say nothing hit Marcia. Please, God. Please, God. Please, God.

He thought he heard Marcia yelling his name.

CHAPTER EIGHT

"Hold still." Someone was pushing him down.

"Got to get to her," Zed punched out with his left fist and felt a satisfying crunch.

"Dammit, how in the hell is he even conscious? Hold him down so I can get some morphine into him."

"Where is she?" Zed croaked out. His head, neck, and right arm felt like they were on fire, and he couldn't see anything, but where was Marcia?

"I'm here. Zed, I'm here." Why did she sound so far away?

He tried to move his right arm again, and when that didn't work, he tried to pull his legs in, so he could kick out.

"Watch it! Strap him down."

Why couldn't he see anything?

"Can you hear me?" It was Marcia's voice.

A woman was screaming. "Marcia, why are you screaming?"

"It isn't me, Zed. It's one of the women from the tourist camp. There are four injured people."

"Alice?" he asked.

"Raymond took Alice on the other helicopter." He could hear the tears in her voice.

"Don't cry."

"Quit trying to talk. Every time you do the bandage on your neck gets bloodier. Why is he still awake?" she said shrilly.

Ah dammit. He'd felt this before. This was not the first time he'd been drugged up when he'd been injured. He tried to force his eyes open again. "Get to Brockman," it was the last words he said, then he was lulled to sleep by the hum of the helicopter.

* * *

Sunlight. Drapes. Flowers.

Well, he wasn't aboard the USS Ronald Reagan that was for damn sure. He must be stateside. Just how bad had he been wounded? It hurt when he turned his head. Didn't stop him though. Might as well start his physical therapy now. He saw Hunter look up from a magazine.

"Aliana's going to be upset that she missed you waking up. She just went to the bathroom."

"So, the flowers aren't from you? I'm hurt."

"Look closer, there are three bouquets. And no, none of them are from me." Then Hunter grimaced and got out of his chair and strode over to the windowsill. "Shit, Alia signed my name to the arrangement she brought."

"Hell Hunter, even I knew that was going to happen."

"You sound like shit." Hunter picked up the glass with the straw and brought it to Zed, so he could take a sip.

"I know I've been told things before. I kind of remember the surgeon talking to me on the Reagan after surgery. But it's vague. Can you fill me in?"

He remembered being on the helicopter. Marcia, she'd been safe. He hadn't been able to see her, but he'd heard her. He'd asked about her when he came out of surgery. They'd laughed because apparently, he'd asked often. She'd been shipped stateside.

"You almost died."

"I didn't, so it doesn't count. Any permanent damage?"

Hunter chuckled. "Isn't your real question, when can you get back to the teams?"

Sometimes it sucked to have people who knew you so well. Zed nodded, then grimaced at the pain.

"No permanent damage. Not even to your vocal chords. However, got to admit, right now, you're sounding kind of sexy."

"Teams?"

"Doc said full recovery, duty ready in four to six weeks. You have some ligament damage on your right shoulder, not to mention your neck is fucked up."

"Didn't know fucked up was a diagnosis."

"Talk to your doctor if you want something more precise. It's your shoulder shit that's going to require rehab."

"Got it," Zed grinned. "Now fill me in on the mission."

The door pushed open, and Aliana Novak, Hunter's soon-to-be-wife stepped into the room. She gave Zed a warm smile. "You're awake. We've been so worried about you." She came up to his bed and adjusted the sheet. "Do you need some water? What can I get you?"

"What do you want to get for me, Alia?" Zed gave her a slow smile, loving the way she blushed.

"Quit giving my fiancé a hard time," Hunter admonished as he walked up and put his arm around Aliana. She stood up straight and shrugged out of Hunter's hold.

"Zed, what I want to get for you is a quick kick in the ass for getting injured and worrying my man."

Zed laughed. He liked this new level of spunk. It reminded him of Marcia. He looked over at Hunter. Now, Marcia he could safely ask about in front of Aliana.

"Where's Marcia? She was injured too."

"She's still in town answering questions," Hunter answered carefully.

"How long have I been here? How many days have they been asking her questions?" Zed pushed himself up on the bed as well as he was able.

"You probably shouldn't move." Aliana rushed forward. "You've only been here since last night."

He continued to prop himself up on his elbows and squint at Hunter. "How long has Marcia been in custody?"

Hunter got up and draped his arm around Aliana. "Zed, get real, she's not in custody. She's nobody's prisoner. She's just answering a few questions."

"How many days?" Zed asked again in a low rumble.

Hunter looked down at Aliana.

"Uhm," Hunter hesitated.

"This is my signal to leave," Aliana sighed softly. "Zed, I'm so glad you're feeling better." She turned to Hunter and kissed his cheek. "Don't wear him out," she said forcefully. "I don't care how much information he wants, he needs his rest."

She headed for the door, and Zed remembered his manners. "Aliana," Zed called out.

She turned and smiled at him. "Yes?"

"Thanks for the flowers."

"It was Hunter's idea," she said as she walked out the door.

"She's been hanging out with the team more, hasn't she?" Zed chuckled wryly.

"Yep. She's turning into a smartass," Hunter grinned broadly.

"Now, tell me, how many days has Marcia been answering questions?"

"What happened out in the jungle between you and Marcia Price?" Hunter countered.

"That's not relevant. Just answers my question." Zed's strength gave out and his head hit the pillow. Hunter leaned over and adjusted the bed, so Zed was in more of a sitting position,

"Is that better?" Hunter asked.

"Answer my goddamn question."

"She's been answering questions since she got stateside which was three days ago. Brockman didn't know what was going on with her because she didn't tell him, and all he cared about was getting home to Virginia, so his youngest daughters could visit him in the hospital there. I'm sure if he was running on all cylinders, he would have put a stop to Homeland Security putting the screws to Marcia."

"Why did they?"

"As soon as she mentioned a man named Jefferies, all bets were off. He's way above our pay grade." Hunter picked up the cup again and started to put the straw to Zed's lips.

"Give that to me."

Hunter chuckled and carefully placed the cup in Zed's hand.

Zed grimaced when his hand trembled as he held the cup and straw one handed up to his mouth. His other damn arm was useless because it was connected to an IV and some kind of space-aged monitoring system. Hunter took the cup back and placed it on the nightstand when Zed was through, then pulled up a chair and sat down.

"I want a report on everyone who was injured."

"Aye aye," Hunter saluted.

Zed just stared at him.

"Brockman was in bad shape by the time he hit the Reagan. He ended up needing a portion of his lung removed. He was in surgery for seven hours whereas you were in surgery for one-and-a-half."

"I saw two people die at the tourist camp."

"Five total."

"Tell me."

"After you were hit, Raymond took the woman who operated the camp as a hostage onto their helicopter. He wanted Marcia who he still thought was Lesley Brockman, but you protected her. So, he took the other woman instead and that was the reason our Seahawk didn't shoot down their Mi helicopter. The only fucking reason. Everyone knew she was going to die, but we just couldn't do it ourselves."

Zed thought back to those moments right before he was hit. He remembered covering Marcia with his body, he remembered shooting, then the bullet slamming into him, and praying nothing had hit the woman under him. He also remembered Raymond still holding Alice by the neck and backing up toward the Mi Helicopter, the fucker.

"I understand why they didn't shoot down the helicopter with Alice on it. It was the right decision." Hunter reached over and plucked the empty glass from Zed's hand. "I remember Marcia on the Seahawk, and there was somebody else crying, another woman's voice. I thought I heard Nurul."

"The native woman?" Hunter asked. "The one with the baby?"

"Yeah, that's her."

"Marcia threw a fit when our guys were going to leave without her. Made them go and get her. There were also four more injured at the camp, one a child who came aboard the

Seahawk and taken to the aircraft carrier. One of the men didn't make it."

"Did you find Alice?"

Hunter rested his elbows on his knees and looked down at the floor.

"Just tell me what happened."

"The pilot of the Seahawk reported he saw a body being thrown from the Mi. They were too far away to do anything, and he was still in the process of taking on wounded."

Both men sat in silence for a while.

"Did we get some kind of idea of where they ended up?" Zed asked.

"They flew too low," Hunter shook his head. "They were headed toward Sandakan. All of our ships were deployed on the Northwest side of Borneo. We have people on the lookout."

Zed knew there were a lot of places the helicopter could land, and there were a lot of inlets along the coast where they could easily get a boat.

"How long was the debriefing?"

"Marcia's was the longest since she spent all that extra time with Felix Raymond. She's due to be on her way home to Virginia tomorrow."

"Where's she going to stay?"

"You still haven't told me what she means to you," Hunter said.

"She is just someone I rescued. Now answer the question."

"Look Zed, I didn't get her life story, okay. I just know that she's due back in Virginia. I heard Brockman's daughters are being taken care of by their aunt and uncle. There was something about an older sister who is in rehab for heroin. I only know this shit because Dex runs his mouth. Okay? If you need more info, go talk to him."

Zed blew out a deep breath. It still didn't tell him what he needed to know about Marcia. He thought she lived with the Brockmans, but he really wasn't sure, and it really bothered him. But why should it?

"Zed, I'm going to ask again, and not just for my edification, but also for you. What does this woman mean to you?"

He looked at this man who was one of his oldest friends and answered honestly, "A lot. She means one hell of a lot. If you ask me why, I couldn't really explain it."

Hunter stared at him for a long minute, then nodded. "I can accept that. You've always been a bit of a spooky bastard."

Zed barked out a laugh. "So how many days before I can blow this popsicle stand?"

Hunter leaned over and hit Zed's call button. "Once the nurse lets your doctor know you're conscious, she'll give you an ETA. I was going to tell you the doctor was hot, but I don't expect that matters anymore, right?"

"You'd be right, it doesn't matter." His focus was elsewhere.

* * *

Marcia disconnected her call. Vi had sounded like her usual upbeat self and was in the process of retiring from her job as a teacher. She would be a great help. She rolled her neck and wondered when the pain would stop. It was either her leg or her head that was hurting, and she'd be damned if she was going to take another one of those prescribed pain pills. Nothing but Tylenol for this girl. But man, she hurt, and the doctor said she could expect this for the next week!

She pushed up from the hotel bed and eyed the clock. She eyed the Uber app on her phone, the car was five minutes away. Based on her hobbling speed, she'd just make it to the lobby in time to meet him. Visiting hours weren't going to last much longer. Too bad Frick and Frack had taken so long with her 'debriefing' today. Just how many times could they ask a question in a different way? You would have thought that she was a criminal or something.

She was so mad, she tried to slam her hotel room door shut, but in the end, she just couldn't bring herself to do it. Somebody might be trying to rest. Then when she started stomping toward the elevator, she just ended up hurting herself.

Yay for team Price, what an idiot.

At least punching the button a bunch of times for the elevator didn't hurt her.

"In a hurry?"

A tall man dressed in a suit was smiling down at her. But it was the wrong tall man. He didn't have dark eyes, high cheekbones or warm caramel skin, and his smile didn't make her melt.

"Just trying to get to the hospital before visiting hours are over with," Marcia answered.

"Family?" he asked.

His voice didn't rumble. He could be quiet any time now as far as she was concerned. She pressed the button again, letting her hair hide her face. "Nope, a friend."

He shut up.

The elevator opened, and they waited in an awkward silence until they got to the lobby, Marcia did her best not to limp as she headed to the front. Her car was waiting. It was good it wasn't cold in San Diego, she only had a light coat. She'd gotten some clothes from someone on the aircraft carrier and a few more here in San Diego. How they had managed to get her ID, bank card, and a replacement phone so fast, she had no idea, but she wasn't just dealing with the military, she was dealing with Homeland Security.

"Lady, are you listening to me? Where to?"

She gave the address for the US Naval hospital she'd memorized.

Now that she was on her way to see Zed, she was nervous. The man was a SEAL, he probably had women throwing themselves at him all the time. What were they called? Buckle Bunnies? Nope, that was for girls who liked the men in the rodeo. Silly Putty! Lesley knew this kind of thing. She always knew things.

Frog Hogs!

Her palms started to sweat. Please say Zed wasn't going to think she was following him around like some swooning woman.

Buckle up, Buttercup. Stop this. Marcia wiped her hands on her jeans and sat up straighter in the back of the car. You don't feel good, and those men hadn't been doing a darn thing for her self-esteem. Why did they question her like she was some kind of conspirator when she'd been a victim? She'd wished Mr. B. hadn't been still in the hospital, he wouldn't have allowed this.

Then there was the fact they wouldn't tell her what had been going on with Nurul. It wasn't until she refused to open her mouth for three hours, they finally told her that Hana was doing fine and recovering. They didn't tell her where though. If it weren't for the fact she needed to see Zed, she would have just taken a flight home today.

"We're here."

She looked around and realized they were in front of the hospital. She dug in her pocket for some bills to tip the man. She didn't even have a purse. She needed to get home. She wanted her own clothes, her own things. But.

Marcia walked into reception. "I'm here to visit Zed Zaragoza." She shifted as they looked on the computer, her leg hurting.

"We don't have a Zed, but we have a Dante Zaragoza, is that who you're looking for?"

"Uhm, yes," Marcia nodded. How many Zaragoza's could there be at the hospital.

"He's on the third floor. Visiting hours are going to be over in an hour," the woman warned her.

"Thank you." Marcia headed for the elevator.

Once again, she pressed the button multiple times. She didn't have much time and wanted to make the most of her time with Zed. Oops, Dante. What the heck? Dante? Oh yeah, he'd introduced himself as Dante in the jungle. That'd seemed like a lifetime ago.

"Hey, there." Strong arms steadied her as she rolled back on her feet. She looked up and for a moment she thought it was Zed. Marcia frowned as she realized that it was another big Hispanic-American man.

"Are you okay?" he asked.

"I'm fine," she smiled tentatively. It was the eyes. Their eyes were the same. "Do you know Zed?" she asked.

"Marcia?" he asked. "I'm Hunter Diaz."

"Zed talked about you," Marcia grinned.

"Let's go on up, I'll show you to his room."

"It's three-twenty-eight, right? I think I can find it on my own," she assured him and stepped around him to enter the elevator. He held it open and pulled out his wallet. What was he doing?

"Take my card," he said. "If you need anything, anything at all, give me a call."

She took it out of his hand. "That's really nice of you, but I'll be fine Hunter."

"You never know. Just think of me as a Zed stand-in until he's up on his feet."

The man might look a little like Zed Zaragoza, but there is no way he could compete. "Yeah sure," Marcia said as she shoved his card into her pants pocket.

He gave her a slow smile that got really wide.

"What?" she asked defensively.

"I'm just thinking, it must have been an interesting time in the jungle."

"Can you let the door go?" she scowled. "There isn't that much time for visiting."

"It was nice meeting you, Ms. Price," Hunter said as he let the door close.

She watched the numbers as they turned over to three and thought about Hunter Diaz. What had all that been about? Well, at least he had been nicer than the suits she'd been dealing with for the last three days. When she got out of the elevator, she hustled down the hall as best she could to Zed's room. His door was closed, so she knocked.

"Come in."

Yep, it was him, she recognized that rumble from her dreams. Her straight white teeth bit into her lower lip as she considered that. What was she doing dreaming about his voice? She shook her head and opened the door. As soon as she saw him, relief poured through her. He was awake, and his black eyes were bright as he looked at her.

"Marcia," he grinned broadly. "I planned to track you down." He held out his hand to her. As if there was a magnet in his hand, and she was made of steel, she grasped it. He pulled her so she fell against him, his strong arm holding her as her face pressed against his cheek.

"Watch out. You're hurt."

"The bandage is on the other side," he said gruffly. He was right, so she nuzzled against his neck, breathing him in. It was stupid. This wasn't the reason she was here. She just wanted to say thank you, but there was no way she was going to leave his embrace.

"Hey. Hey. Are you okay?"

Darn it. She was getting his neck wet. She tried to pull away, but his arm held her in place. "Let me go."

"Marcia, what is it?"

She pulled up enough, so she could look into his eyes. "I'm just emotional. It was a lot, you know?"

"Explain it to me," he requested softly.

"I should have died at least five thousand times, but you saved me."

"The way I remember it, you saved yourself. And you saved Nurul and Hana. You're a hero."

She bit her lip, and his eyes flickered down to watch, then raised to look her in the eye. "I wanted to see you. Thanks for coming," Zed said.

"I needed to see you." She shuddered. "I needed to see if you were real."

He seemed to be saying so much with his eyes, but maybe she was reading it wrong. She couldn't stand it. She needed to lighten the mood.

"Dante, huh?"

"Occasionally. Depends on the circumstances." His voice went through her like liquid heat. He couldn't possibly mean what she thought he did. Was his hand squeezing her waist a little tighter?

"How are you?" His hand came up to trace the curve of her cheek. "I can barely see the bruising on your face, so that's good. But you were limping when you came in, how's your leg? Your head?"

"I'm fine."

"Marcia, you'd say you were fine if you were on fire."

She snorted a laugh.

"So, tell me the truth, what did the doctors say?"

"I got the all clear on the concussion. My leg is infection free, that was their big worry."

"But?" he prompted.

"They recommended R.I.C.E."

"Sounds really familiar," Zed chuckled. "Rest, ice, compression, and elevation."

"Yep, that's it. The swelling has gone down, but I'm still limping. They said the week after next, I should be back to normal."

"Hunter told me Homeland Security has been questioning you. How hard of a time have they been giving you?"

She sighed, it was time for business. "Not a hard time, exactly," she prevaricated.

"Bullshit. Three days? They've been questioning you for three fucking days?"

Marcia pressed up against his chest and reluctantly, left the comfort of his embrace. She sat down in the chair beside the bed. "Okay, three days was overkill. I don't know what their problem was either. They treated me like I was on trial or something. I had to tell them over and over again everything Raymond ever said."

"That should have taken three hours," Zed said as he leaned forward and speared her with a fierce glance.

"I agree," she grinned. "But I made them work for it."

"What do you mean?"

"It was actually after four hours, I gave them the silent treatment."

"You asked for a lawyer?"

"Nope," she smiled broadly, remembering the two agents' frustration and eventual fury.

"You're killing me here, Marcia, I see your smile, and it's absolutely diabolical. What in the hell did you do?"

"Nurul and Hana had been left behind in Borneo. I told them until they got her on the phone with a translator, I wasn't going to talk to them again. That's part of the reason I was there so long," she admitted.

Zed shouted with laughter. "How is Nurul? How's the baby?"

"They're with Nurul's auntie. The doctor on the aircraft carrier made sure Hana's arm was set properly, and they had gotten her back to her family. She's still really tore up about her dad."

"It's not your fault," Zed reiterated what he'd said in the jungle.

"She's going to be staying with her aunt. I took down all of her contact information. I'm going to send them some funds."

"Marcia," Zed frowned, "you don't have to mother the Western Hemisphere." He held out his hand, and she reached out and took it. He made her feel less alone. How funny was that? She had more people in her life than most.

"It's not a big deal, Zed. With their cost of living, they don't need much, and I get interest payouts every year from my parent's life insurance policies. That's what paid for my college."

He just shook his head. "So that's why it took three days to question you, huh?"

"Not entirely. Day three was spent asking all the same questions they asked on day one. It was stupid. They really ticked me off. They were A-Holes."

Zed's lips twitched.

"What?"

"Has it worked? Do Brockman's two younger daughters not swear?"

"No," Marcia sighed, "both of them have potty mouths, sometimes. It really yanks my chain."

"How about when grown men swear?" Zed asked carefully.

"I couldn't care less," Marcia grinned. "I'm just about setting an example. However, I will say I would prefer the adults try to keep it clean around the kids." Marcia waited to see how Zed would take that, and she didn't have to wait long.

"I agree. That's part of what we do in the military, set an example."

She thought about it. She'd been to bars in Virginia when she'd gone out with Rick, and some of the military guys had been pretty rowdy and rude. But then again, how many times had she been out walking around campus or just seeing the sights and come across some of the politest men and women possible?

"What are you thinking?" Zed asked.

"I'm thinking people are people," she answered. "Good, bad, and indifferent, they come in all flavors. I went to Virginia State, and not all the military I ran into were setting an example, but then again, many were. I guess I was just painting a lot of people with the same brush."

"You live in Alexandria now, don't you?"

"How did you know?"

"We were briefed on everybody who was on the yacht. Just the basics. But it made it sound like you were living with the Brockman family."

"I am. Ever since Mrs. B. died, I've been living there. It dovetailed with when I graduated."

"So, you're the girl's nanny?"

Marcia started to giggle. Zed scowled at her, and that made her really start to laugh.

"What's so damn funny?"

"I have a B.S. in Mathematics. I'm currently working as a junior economist at JP Morgan. The C.I.A. wanted me to work as an intern."

"Thank God, you turned them down."

"Why?"

"Once they realized the type of woman you were, they'd have you in the field in an instant. It'd scare the hell out of me."

"You don't think I'm capable?" She held her breath as she waited for his answer.

"Didn't you hear me? They'd be crazy not to have you in the field, you'd be excellent. My hair would go white overnight."

She leaned closer. His raven black hair was cut short, but she could see just a bit of a curl on the ends. "There's not a bit of gray," she protested.

His black eyes turned liquid. "I hadn't met you."

Marcia's breath held. He hadn't really said that, had he? He didn't mean anything by it, did he?

"I'm temporarily assigned here in San Diego. I have about five more months here before I return to my team in Virginia," he said seriously.

"You live in Virginia?" she breathed.

He nodded his head. "Small world, huh?"

She smiled slowly.

He gave her that wicked grin she remembered from the jungle. "Don't make any dates before I get back into town. Consider your dance card full. I've already arranged with Amelia to transfer some of my physical therapy time back to Walter Reed."

"You'll be in Virginia?" she grinned. "When?"

"Three weeks, so you can consider me booked up until that time."

"How'd you know what I was going to ask?"

"I just knew."

CHAPTER NINE

Buy flowers. Pick up Christie from ballet. E-mail the report to Ms. Franklin. What was she forgetting? Oh yeah, hit the mall, so she could get some of Lesley's favorite bath bombs and the cashmere blanket, how could she have forgotten?

"Excited much?" she asked herself.

Marcia admitted she was both excited and scared. This was the third time Lesley had been in rehab, and she was praying the third time was the charm. It did seem different, for one it was longer, and two, Lesley had already worked out a plan for aftercare which she had never done before.

She'd even called Marcia and told her to get rid of all the sweets in the house. That was the reason she hadn't baked a cake. Please God, please God, please God say this time it was going to be different. Thinking about Lesley's aftercare reminded Marcia she needed to prod Mr. B. to call Debbie's psychologist. She really thought they might need to up the appointments from one to two a week. Borneo still had its grips on the young girl.

Marcia pulled into the mall parking garage and couldn't find one single spot until she reached the top level which is where she parked her little Honda. An hour. You need to be at ballet in an hour, so get your ass in gear. She practically ran to the entrance. She wanted to get things done in forty-five minutes, so she could call back Zed and find out exactly when his plane was going to land in three days.

Shopping was a blur. She was just happy she wasn't snarky to the lady in front of her at the beauty and bath store who insisted on telling the clerk her life story when making a five-dollar purchase. She was still thinking about that when she scooted past the white van parked perpendicular to her car.

"Marcia?"

Her blood ran cold. She looked up and saw Raymond's arm reaching out toward her as another man started to open up the side door of the van. How did he know her real name?

"Rape!" she screamed at the top of her lungs and started running.

She didn't see anyone, not one single person. Her head swung wildly. Stairs? Elevator? Ramp? Definitely ramp.

"Rape!" she kept screaming and running.

Marcia saw stars when she hit the pavement. A big body was on top of her. Then she felt a hand covering her mouth, her nose. She couldn't breathe. She shook her head back and forth, trying to work the hand loose. When it moved, she took a bite.

"Motherfucker!"

He slammed her head into the pavement.

"I've called the police," a woman yelled.

Marcia felt herself hauled up off the ground. Raymond was going to take her. Over her dead body. She struggled like mad, clawing, kicking, she turned her head to bite.

"I've got a gun, if you don't let her go, I'll shoot," the woman sounded resolute.

She heard a shot, then another.

A muffled scream, then the sound of tires squealing and getting closer.

"Don't think you're getting away, Girly." Marcia saw the van beside her. Oh God, Raymond was trying to push her in. She grabbed the side. No, she wasn't going. She wasn't. Her face met cement.

Was that a siren?

* * *

He was getting pretty damn sick of seeing her face bruised and scraped. Marcia looked so damn tiny in the hospital bed.

"I don't think we've met before," the older man said as he got up out of the reclining chair in the corner of the hospital room.

"Zed Zaragoza," he said as he held out his hand.

The man nodded. "Harold Brockman. I haven't heard enough about you, Master Chief."

"Something tells me, you've read a lot about me though."

"You'd be right." He set down the book he'd been reading.

"How is Marcia doing?" Zed asked. "I came as soon as I heard."

"About that, how did you hear?"

"Kane McNamara, he's a member of Night Storm, his specialty is—"

"I know what his specialty is," Brockman interrupted. "My department tried to recruit him a couple of years ago. So, you had him watching Marcia, did you? Did you think Raymond would come after her? And if you did why in the hell didn't you give me a heads up?" his tone turned to ice.

"I didn't think Raymond would come after her, Sir. If I did, you can be damn sure I would have had ensured she was protected," Zed said with calm authority. "I expect you and I are going to be kicking ourselves for years we didn't see this coming." Zed noted Brockman's flinch.

"Yes, I will," he agreed. "That still doesn't tell me why you had her under surveillance."

"Not under surveillance. Just had her flagged so if anything came up, I would be notified. As soon as the police report came in, I had a copy and was making my flight arrangements."

"I heard something about her dance card being full?" Brockman gave a half smile.

"I'm taking her back to San Diego with me as soon as she's discharged from the hospital."

The man's smile disappeared. "You are not."

"Yes, I am. You don't want to put your family at risk."

"Marcia is part of my family," Brockman said tightly.

"Look, I'm not trying to be an ass about this, but you live with two minors, and Marcia's been damned worried about Lesley coming home. It doesn't sound like she's in any shape to take on the stress of having twenty-four/seven guards."

"Even if Marcia goes with you, my family is still going to have round-the-clock protection."

Zed rubbed his neck and rolled his stiff right shoulder. "Sir—"

"Call me Harold."

Zed nodded. "Harold, we need to get to the bottom of why Raymond still wants someone close to you. Is it money? Is it to blackmail you for information? What? But whatever it is, I think we can both agree on one thing."

"What's that?"

"Marcia bested him in Borneo. You read his file. He hates women. Marcia is now his target to get to whatever he wants. Now, Harold, what does he want?"

"It's not him, it's Jefferies," Brockman sighed. "He used to work with me at the NSA. He was on assignment in Beirut and supposedly died in a car bomb. When Marcia said Raymond mentioned him, we knew we were in trouble."

"So, Raymond has focused on Marcia to get to you because he's a sociopath, and he's the conduit Jefferies has employed. That still doesn't tell me what Jefferies wants."

"The projects we worked together on are complete. He shouldn't know about the things I'm doing now I've retired."

Zed gave a grim laugh. Even though there were plenty of things that should be above his pay grade, it didn't mean he wasn't able to piece together what was going on, and he was a grunt compared to Jefferies.

Brockman flushed. "I know," he said. "Unfortunately, nothing is sacrosanct. When it was just Raymond and some of the others, I thought it was revenge for the screw-up with the Saudi palace, but as soon as Jefferies was mentioned, I realized it has to be the Malaysian cult or the fissionable material."

"What's your best guess?"

"I have my men looking into it."

Zed stared at him, then finally nodded. He didn't tell him, but he was still going to have Dex and Kane work on it as well.

"So, it's agreed, Marcia is coming with me."

"Son, nothing was agreed," Brockman protested.

Again, Zed stared at him. Brockman gave it one last shot. "You could be deployed."

"You forget, I'm still recovering. I won't be mission ready for another five weeks. I'm doing PT at this point. Her little butt is going to be glued to a chair next to me."

"She's not going to go for it."

"How do you plan to keep her here, guilt?"

Brockman's eyes narrowed. "What do you mean by that?"

"If Marcia thinks she's needed, you can manipulate her to do anything even if it isn't in her own best interests. Has living with you for the last two years been the right thing for her?"

In the last four weeks, Zed had talked to Marcia on the phone ten times. He'd gotten a pretty good idea of what made her tick, and her heart often overwhelmed her own self-interests.

"You have no idea the blow that little bastard Rick Parsons was on her self-esteem, she needed a safe spot to land," Brockman said defensively.

"Really? Seems to me, she went from the frying pan into the fire. I understand her being there for your family after your wife died was the right thing, but two years?" Zed raised his eyebrow.

Brockman's face turned red. Then he walked over to where Marcia rested and looked at her for long moments. He came back to face Zed.

"She makes it so easy. My God, there's nobody like her. I was a mess after Margaret died, and then Lesley turning to opioids, then to heroin. You can't imagine." Zed flinched at the man's words. "Christie and Debbie soaked in Marcia's love when I just wasn't emotionally available. I didn't see how selfish I was."

Zed put his hand on Brockman's shoulder and squeezed.

"I'm going to make this right." Zed's eyes twinkled, and Brockman saw it.

"What are you looking so smug about?"

"I had a bet with myself, and I now get to buy a new snowboard."

"You knew I was going to rectify things with Marcia? How?"

"I've read your books. The man who wrote *The Road To Peace* couldn't help but try to do the right thing." Zed looked over his shoulder at Marcia and smiled softly. "She's not going to go willingly, and I would hate for your role as her surrogate father to suffer."

"Zed, this is my mess, I'll straighten it out. I'm more than capable of taking it on the chin." Zed didn't think the man was aware he was rubbing his chin as he said it.

"Yeah, but you trying to convince her won't be expedient. It will take too much time." Zed thought through various scenarios, discarding many until a plan began to coalesce. "I'm just going to take her."

"How do you plan to get an unwilling woman on a plane?"

"Good old-fashioned emotional blackmail."

* * *

She jerked awake. It was one of those helpless jarring movements your body makes that is so disconcerting. Marcia's eyes slammed open to bright lights, and she felt defenseless and exposed. She turned her head back and forth trying to see where she was and who was with her.

"Easy," a low familiar rumble came from her left. Her hand was gently squeezed. "You're with friends, *Querida*."

Just that easily her fright eased.

"Zed?" she croaked.

"I'm here." The bright lights were dimmed, and she could see his face.

"Who else is here?"

"I'm here too, Marcia," a familiar voice whispered. Lesley Brockman peered over Zed's shoulder.

Marcia reared up in the bed, then let out a shrill cry of pain which Lesley echoed. Zed was there to help guide her back down onto the hospital bed.

"I need you to stay down, okay?"

"What's wrong?" Lesley whimpered.

"It's going to be all right, okay ladies?" Marcia calmed at Zed's soothing voice, it gave her something to cling too. "Lesley, right now your friend has just managed to get into a spot of trouble again which has resulted in a ton of bruising, scrapes, and a concussion. If she could have, I'm sure somehow she would have managed to have found a python at the mall too."

"Stop it, Zed, it hurts to laugh," Marcia laughed.

"What do you mean a python?" Lesley asked.

"It's a long story," Marcia sighed. "What are you two doing here? What time is it?"

"Don't you mean what day is it?" Zed asked wryly.

Marcia's eyes widened. She looked over at Lesley and swallowed. "You came home on Friday. What day is it, Lesley?"

She stepped around Zed to the top of the bed. She pushed back some of Marcia's unruly curls and kissed her forehead. "It's Monday."

She felt it then and hated it. Stupid weak tears. Raymond had stolen three days from her. They were gone. "How was your welcome home party?"

Lesley glanced over at Zed. "You know she's serious, don't you?" She turned back to Marcia and raised her voice. "How could you even ask something so stupid? You were almost kidnapped? We didn't have my damned party. You were the important one. You!" Lesley burst into tears.

Marcia held out her arms, and Lesley fell into her embrace. It was a familiar pattern. "Lesley, I've been so worried about you. I'm so glad you're home. How are you, honey?" Lesley hiccupped as Marcia stroked her brown curls.

"I was so scared when Daddy told me what had happened to all of you. Then to find out the nightmare wasn't over," her body trembled against Marcia.

"Are you seeing your counselor?" Marcia asked quietly.

"Yes," she said as she grabbed a tissue from the nightstand and blew her nose. It took long minutes for Lesley to calm down. In the meantime, Marcia missed the feel of Zed holding her hand. Looking up at his hooded gaze, she realized she couldn't get a read on what he was thinking. It was weird, in the jungle she'd felt really in tune with the man.

"Lesley," Zed said quietly. "Why don't you go tell your father Marcia is awake?"

Lesley pulled out of her arms, wiping her tears with the sleeve of her shirt. "Dad's down in the cafeteria. He had some calls to make. He'll be so happy to see you. He's been here every day."

"It would be great to see him. I love you, Lesley, it's great seeing *you*," Marcia said pointedly.

"Yeah well…" Lesley shrugged. She ducked her head instead of looking at Zed and left the room.

"Now, tell me what happened," Marcia demanded. "Everything is kind of a blur. I heard gunshots. Did Raymond kill more people?"

"Actually, there was a woman on the scene who had a license to carry a concealed weapon. She was a former Marine. She shot and killed the man who was working with Raymond. He had a record a mile long." Marcia breathed a sigh of relief.

"Nothing bad is going to happen to her, is it?"

"No, there are video cameras in the mall parking garage, she's in the clear."

"When can I leave here?"

"Just as soon as you're good to fly."

She shifted in the bed so she could see him a little better because something must be wrong with her hearing.

"You heard me just fine," he said.

"Quit reading my mind, it's irksome."

"I've never heard anyone use the word irksome before," Zed chuckled.

"Get used to it, SEAL-boy. What the hell do you mean do you mean I have to be ready to fly?" But she knew exactly what he meant. He thought she was going to go back to San Diego with him. The darn man had another think coming. There was no way she was just going to turn tail and run because of one little incident.

"You know what I mean," he said calmly.

"And just what makes you think that I'm going to just dance to your tune?"

"Are you really going to put Christie and Debbie at risk? I watched the surveillance tapes. It was clear as day Raymond said 'Marcia' not 'Lesley.' This isn't about getting the Brockman daughters anymore. He has a vendetta against you. Are you really going to put those two little girls in the line of fire?"

"Why is he doing this Zed?" All stiffness left her shoulders, the fire was gone. "I don't get it."

"The man is a whack-job."

"There has to be something in it for him. He still has to want to get to Mr. B. through me, and if he does, why not his real daughters?"

Zed skooched up the chair so he could put his arm around her. "*Querida*, you know Brockman cares about you the same way he does his own flesh and blood."

She shook her head. Ow. She shouldn't have done that. Zed pressed a kiss to her temple and she melted. Looking up into his warm eyes, she could see they were the darkest chocolate.

"Don't do that."

"Don't do what? Don't claim what is mine?"

Marcia shivered. Then scowled. "I'm not a 'what,' I'm a woman."

Zed threw back his head and laughed.

"We are going to have so much fun together."

CHAPTER TEN

Two days ago, they'd had a rip-roaring fight at the Brockman's house when he'd insisted she pack. Harold had been smart enough to get him and his daughters out of the line of fire.

"I'm only packing one suitcase because I'm only going to be gone one week. There's absolutely no way I'm going to be gone any longer. The girls need me. Lesley needs me. Mr. B. needs me. You're lucky I agreed to a week, and I only did that because Mr. B. made such a compelling argument."

She didn't even come up to his chin, but it didn't stop her from going head-to-head with him.

"Suit yourself, but I thought women liked more changes of clothes for five weeks."

"And if I was staying five weeks, I would pack more," she said sweetly. Marcia even batted her long eyelashes. Zed leaned against her bedroom wall and pretended she wasn't getting to him.

"Harold's already sent a note from the hospital to your supervisor saying you need five weeks to recover. He's arranged to have his sister stay for the next five weeks. I'd say you've been outmaneuvered."

She paused mid-fold of the red lingerie in her hand and looked at him. Her eyes glinted. "Well, I guess that means I get to take a vacation. I'm thinking Paris."

Yep, she was fired up. Zed couldn't take his eyes off the crimson silk she was taking her time folding and putting into the suitcase. She was doing it on purpose.

Zed grinned. "Well, if your passport is in order…"

"They reissued it after the mess in Borneo." She strode over to her dresser and rummaged through the jewelry box. After a moment, she carefully closed the lid and turned to Zed.

"Paris, Texas," she carefully enunciated. "I'm going on vacation in Paris, Texas after I'm done with my week in San Diego."

Zed pushed away from the wall and went to Marcia. He took her clenched fists in his hands and brought them to his lips. "Is it really such a hardship to go home with me?"

"It is when I'm going with you under duress."

That floored him. "What are you talking about?"

"The big bad SEAL is going to take care of the little woman." Her eyes were overly bright, and her lower lip quivered just the slightest before she bit it and jutted out her chin. There she was, her face bruised and raw, and she was defiant as hell. Was it any wonder he was so enamored?

He captured both of her hands in one and gently stroked her cheek. "You know better than that, Mi Corazón. We were just *biding our time until I could come back home to Virginia. But you are correct about one thing, it is my right to protect you."*

She glared at him and opened her mouth, but he pressed his thumb against her lips.

"Wait. I have a question for you. If it were in your power to protect Christie and Debbie, would you?"

Her warm breath caressed his thumb. "Yes," she sighed. "Okay, you win. I guess the Pacific Ocean beats out Paris, Texas, anyway."

"Maybe I can offer more of an incentive than that," Zed said as he bent down.

Marcia tried to shrug away from him. "I look like doo-doo."

"Stop with the potty mouth, already, it makes me hot and bothered." It did too, he couldn't think of anything about this woman that didn't excite him. Her delicate build could barely contain her indomitable spirit, and Zed was careful as he pulled her close. He swept his hand down her back, and she arched up against him, wresting her wrists out of his grasp. As soon as he let go, she thrust her fingers into his hair and pulled him close for a kiss. Zed hesitated. He looked into her glittering sherry-colored eyes to ensure that she wanted this as much as he did.

"I do," she said as she read his mind. "I need your kiss."

He looked at her mouth, her bottom lip still swollen. He feathered his tongue against the hurt flesh, and she whimpered. She tasted so good, wild and sweet. Marcia parted her lips, just a little, tempting him to tread further. Zed slid deeper, sampling her plump lips as he caressed the lithe line of her back until she began to undulate against him. Her mouth opened as her breasts pressed against his chest. How had he gone from zero to sixty in zero seconds?

Mother of God! The tight swell of Marcia's nipples prodded his chest as she suckled his tongue and made him almost forget his name. Almost.

Zed pulled back and rested his forehead against hers, his breath labored.

"Zed?" He heard the little waver of uncertainty in her voice.

"Dios Mio, *I have never been so aroused by one kiss in my life. Not even with Teresa Gomez when I was thirteen.*" For all Marcia's fire and confidence, Zed could still see her doubt.

"Really?" she asked.

"Really," he assured her. "Marcia, I was thirteen. She let me touch her ta-tas. I'm telling you, you pack a punch." He pushed a lock of her unruly hair behind her ear.

"Now who's talking kid-safe?"

"I was thirteen and raised by my mom and my abuela. I thought ta-ta was a bad word," Zed grinned down at her. "So, can I help you pack more than one suitcase?"

"I suppose."

"I'll start with your lingerie."

Looking at her asleep in his bed, Zed couldn't help but think she was the most beautiful woman in the world. It didn't matter that there were still scabs where she had been pulled along the rough cement.

Forty-five minutes ago, when they'd arrived from the airport, he'd shown her this guest room and maybe he had referred to the bed as 'his' bed. God, he loved getting her riled. She'd gone on to explain it wasn't his bed, it was the guest bed. Zed grinned.

It was a bed in his apartment, wasn't it? Then it was his bed. He wasn't going to get into the semantics of the furniture being rented for the duration of his temporary assignment because then, she'd really argue with him. His woman really liked to argue.

Now that he knew she looked comfortable, Zed went into the kitchen and grabbed a bottle of Gatorade. He knew Marcia would likely be out for a couple of hours, so he'd wait to start dinner. He'd learned a lot about her during their phone conversations. He knew leaving work for five weeks wouldn't be a hardship, her work bored her. Marcia was itching to go back to school and get her Masters.

He grabbed his cell phone and went out on the small balcony to give Gray a call. He owed him one.

"Glad you're back, Zaragoza. How are you feeling?"

Zed rolled his right shoulder, wishing he could say he was at one hundred percent. "I'm feeling pretty good. I'm sure Jackson will make me feel like shit tomorrow."

Gray laughed. The physical therapist on base was not known for being easy, but she got results, and that was all the SEALs cared about. "How's Max?" Gray asked, referring to Max Hogan the lieutenant of his regular team, Night Storm.

"He's doing good. The whole team is. We had a four-star dinner together."

"Mess hall?" Gray guessed.

"Close. Hospital cafeteria," Zed smiled. It had been Leo Perez who had arranged it. He was the glue who kept Night Storm together. Of course, Kane was going to stop by no matter what, he wanted to get a look at Marcia, he had a damn good idea what she meant to Zed.

"How's our patient?" Gray asked.

"Out like a light."

"Should she have been flying today?" Gray sounded concerned. Zed took a sip of his drink, so he didn't say the first thing that came to mind. After a moment he responded.

"She got an all-clear to travel before she left, Lieutenant."

There was a pause. "Sorry about that, Zed. That was out of line, of course, you wouldn't have her travel if it wasn't safe."

Zed continued to drink his Gatorade and look out over the arroyo. "I'm going to want to talk to some of your team about helping me keep an eye on Marcia."

"Goddammit, Zed, I said I was sorry," Gray bit out. "As long as you're here and working with us, Black Dawn is *our* team. You got that?"

Zed relaxed. "I've got it."

"So, are you going to stop calling me Lieutenant?"

"Gray," Zed chuckled, "I was actually hoping to rope you in on this."

"Just try to stop me."

* * *

Marcia couldn't believe there had been actual fizzy bath bombs in a bowl in the bathroom. It had to have been Lesley's idea.

But Zed implemented it.

It was so decadent. When was the last time she'd taken a bath? Let alone with a bath bomb? Marcia climbed into the tub, rested her head against a towel, and closed her eyes.

As the ball swirled around the tub and fizzed, she thought about Lesley. Sometimes, she thought she was looking at a taller and prettier version of herself. These days she was only taller. The drugs had ravaged her. How could she have left Lesley? It about killed her to leave Christie and Debbie. Christie was a bundle of joy, and Debbie was turning into a moody, snarky teenager who was either making her laugh or making her want to strangle her.

Dang nabbit, she was crying. It had just been last week she'd found Debbie in Christie's bed. Out of everything, that was what killed her the most, leaving Debbie. Intellectually, she knew the girl was in good hands. She was seeing a really good psychologist and her aunt Vi was a retired school teacher.

"But I should be with her," Marcia whispered to herself.

She sunk lower in the tub and tried to just let her mind calm. When she did, she realized how much her body hurt. Her actual bones ached. She hated hurting and being a wuss. She'd done track and soccer, how many injuries had there been? Suck it up!

Marcia raised her leg and saw where the python had bitten her. It was going to leave a scar. Borneo was different from the soccer field. She let her leg slide back under the water and closed her eyes, but all she saw was the green of the jungle, and she shuddered. She totally got why Debbie was having nightmares.

"No!" she said hoarsely. "Think of something different."

Marcia sank deeper into the tub, but when her scraped chin hit the frothy water, it stung. It was one of the scabs. Come on, it was just a little Mall Mishap. Pull up those bootstraps. She looked up at the bathroom ceiling and blinked rapidly. She was sick of pulling up her bootstraps. How many years had she been doing it?

Her chin trembled. Mom and Dad. That horrible night when Mr. and Mrs. Brockman had come over to her house with the policeman to tell her that her parents had been in a car accident. Her life had ended that night. She'd been the same age as Debbie when her life had ended, or at least, that was the way she'd felt. Mr. and Mrs. B. had taken her across the street and put her to bed in their house, and she didn't leave until college.

At first, she'd walked around shell-shocked. It took her about six months to realize what was going on. Then it was something Lesley said about her being lucky she'd been taken in since she didn't have any relatives. In hindsight, Marcia could see things clearly, it was just something one fifteen-year-old girl would say to another. At the time? It flipped a switch in Marcia.

She did everything she could to be indispensable to the Brockman's. She babysat, she cleaned, she cooked. But Margaret Brockman saw through everything and did her best to stop Marcia's frantic attempts to assure her place in their home. But it was impossible to get through to her. And if Marcia were to be perfectly honest, trying to please, being a caretaker was an ingrained part of her nature, it always had been. But the near mania was new.

Her parents had left her financially cared for, so she could attend Virginia State and live on campus. Marcia went for it, with some coaxing from Mrs. B.

"Honey, it's going to kill me to have you away from me, but it's only an hour, and I expect constant visits," Margaret Brockman had said.

The Brockman's really had become surrogate parents and had done their best to stop her from taking on too much of a caretaking role, but it had been impossible. Looking back on things, Marcia knew that was why Mrs. B. had coaxed her to live on campus.

Then there had been the Rick debacle. She'd gone home a lot the first two years, but classes got intensive her junior year, so she needed to buckle down and found herself staying at school more and more. Then she and a girlfriend had rented an apartment, and she'd met Rick. Who knew she was considered an easy mark? A mark!

It's not like he'd been the best-looking guy or anything, but he'd been so attentive and caring in the beginning, and she'd soaked it up like a flower soaked up the sun. He made her feel like she was the center of his world. When her roommate had decided to move out, Rick had moved in. Marcia had no reservations, she overlooked anything and everything because for the first time since her parents had died, she had someone in her life who made her feel totally loved.

Rick didn't cook, he didn't clean, he didn't pay for anything, and when he made love to her, it didn't feel all that good, but he listened, and he cared. He did the things that really mattered in a relationship.

Close to the end of her senior year, class had let out early on a Thursday. She'd gotten an A on her statistics class and wanted to cook Rick chicken Florentine to celebrate. He was in their bedroom on his cell phone.

"Jim, I can't play poker this weekend. I need to spend it with Marcia."

She felt so good hearing that.

"I'm pussy whipped all the way to the bank. Let's do it next Thursday instead. I'll just tell her I need money for my car payment." He laughed. *"Fuck yeah it's paid for. She doesn't know though. Man, I've got it so good, I'm going to marry her. Hell, I'm going to suggest we go house hunting next month."*

He paused while Marcia did everything she could not to drop the bag of groceries she was holding.

"Jim, not only that, I'm passing all of my classes because she does my homework. It couldn't get any better."

She went back out the front door and came back in, making a lot of noise.

"Hey Babe, you're home early. How did your statistics class go?"

"I got an A."

"Marcia, you amaze me. What's in the bag?"

She finished out the school year. She put off looking at a house and became more and more distant with Rick. He finally got the message and went on to greener pastures. There never was any kind of confrontation. She graduated. She'd been in the process of applying for jobs when she'd gotten the call that Mrs. B. had collapsed from a brain embolism. Two days later, she was dead. She moved back in with the Brockman's. They needed her.

Once again, Marcia had been dealt a devastating loss, but this time, she couldn't show it. She was dealing with three daughters who had lost their mother and one man who had lost the love of his life. There was no time for her to be upset. She rolled up her sleeves and dove in. Ultimately, she failed.

Lesley got in a car wreck. She and a couple of friends had been drinking, but still, she'd sustained a back injury. They'd prescribed painkillers for a couple of months. Handling Christie and Debbie, Marcia had missed the signs that Lesley was using the drugs as an emotional crutch to deal with her mother's death. So had Mr. B. because he was involved in all sorts of other projects as a coping mechanism.

By the time Marcia realized Lesley was abusing heroin, it was too late. She struggled to maintain the household and shield the younger girls from Lesley's addiction. Marcia wanted to ensure Christie and Debbie had all the love that Mrs. B. would have given them. It wasn't a hardship because they returned it.

Then things had blown up, Lesley had disappeared. It had been a horrifying time. Eventually, she'd come home, and there had been the first trip to rehab. Through it all, Marcia had done her best to maintain a home for Mr. B. and the girls. Then there had been the second bout of rehab. Mr. B. seemed to be finally coming out of his stupor, but for Lesley, it seemed to be too little, too late.

After she came out of rehab for the second time, things were precarious, and she disappeared again. It was the third time she went in for help that Mr. B. went on the speaking tour and took Marcia and the girls with him, and they went on that fateful yacht trip.

She wondered what would have happened if Borneo had never happened. Would she just have drifted and stayed with the Brockman's? She loved those girls. She loved taking care of them, but they weren't her daughters, and she realized she didn't have a life of her own. She'd been wanting something more. That was why she took the job at JP Morgan.

Then all choice had been taken out of her hands after the Mall Mishap. She'd sat stunned in Mr. B.'s study.

"*Marcia, I adore you. You literally saved my sanity when Margaret died. I don't know what Christie, Debbie, and Lesley would have done without you. But I've been a selfish bastard, and I'm ashamed.*"

Were those tears in his eyes?

"*That's not true. You and your wife took me in after Mom and Dad died. It was almost like I had a second set of parents.*"

Harold Brockman looked at her and gave her a sad smile. "That was true when you were fourteen and Margaret was alive.

We treated you like one of our own and did everything we could to nurture you. Especially Margaret."

"And I loved you for it. I will do anything to pay you back for that," she cried.

He looked down at her kindly. "And that's where I've failed you. Somehow I've made you feel you need to pay us back for something that was our privilege."

"I'm saying this wrong. I'm making you feel bad," she protested.

"No, Sweetheart, you're not making me feel bad. I'm the one in the wrong. I was the adult, and I took advantage of your sweet nature. After college, you should have never moved back in with us, you should have moved on and lived your own life."

What was he saying? "Mr. B., I'd just broken up with Rick, and the girls' mother had just died. We all needed one another. You didn't swoop in and force me to take care of things, it worked out perfectly the way it was supposed to." She couldn't stand it a second longer. She threw her arms around her surrogate father. "I love you. If you've taken advantage, then so have I," she sniffed.

Long moments later he eased her out of his arms. "Thank you, Marcia. You are a wonder. Now I'm kicking you out."

"I don't understand."

"You're going with Zed to San Diego. It's safe there. Raymond has his sights on you. He knows where you live. Zed is going to watch you twenty-four/seven."

She sat there stunned. It made no sense. "Mr. B., you and the girls need me. Lesley's coming home, I have to be here for her."

"Vi is going to be here tonight. She's going to be staying for a couple of months."

"Months? How long do you think I'm going to be gone?" she whispered.

He held onto her shoulders. "You're always welcome here." He didn't continue.

Now she felt like she was going to cry. "You don't want me?"

"Marcia, you're one of my daughters. Know that. Believe that. And as one of my daughters, I'm telling you that you have done more than your fair share, and I want you to be happy and live your own life. I love you."

He held her while she cried. Finally, she stepped back and narrowed her eyes. "I'll get an apartment close to my office."

"No, you're going to San Diego," he said firmly.

"Whose bright idea was this?"

"Zed's."

She hadn't believed him. It wasn't until Zed had followed her up to her room to watch her pack, she'd realized it was really happening. And now here she was. Naked. In his apartment. In a cloud of purple fizz.

She heard his footsteps outside the door.

"Do I have to knock? Or do you hear me out here?"

"I hear you. What do want?" Darn it, did she still have to sound petulant?

She heard Zed's soft laughter. "Still kicking and screaming I see."

"You better not be able to see me," she growled.

He laughed louder. "How do you want your steak cooked?"

"I'm a vegan," she lied.

"You are so full of shit."

"Medium."

"Rosé? Merlot? Cabernet or Syrah?"

She sat up so fast in the bath, the towel behind her head fell into the tub. "What did you just ask me?"

"I asked you what your wine choice was. Or did you want something else?"

Dang, no man had that kind of selection of wine hanging around just to impress some woman, he must like wine. Dante 'Zed' Zaragoza liked wine, her inner child sang. Wait a second, let's test this.

"Do you have a wine cooler?" He didn't reply. "I can't hear you Zed."

"Marcia, don't yank my chain."

She rubbed her hands together in glee.

"Surprise me," she called out. Then she grabbed the towel, so she could climb out of the tub. Marcia took her time getting ready. It wasn't quite time for the red bra and panty set, or was it? Oh, what the hell, wasn't the SEAL team motto to be prepared? She rifled through the blue suitcase and tried to decide between the sundress or the shorts and camisole.

Make up your damn mind, Price.

She went with the shorts and camisole. She knew the red of the bra strap would show.

Bad Marcia.

She ran back down the hall and into the bathroom, so she could look in the mirror.

There wasn't a damn thing she could do about her hair. She desperately needed a cut to layer all her curls, but when had she had time to do that? Hopefully, he liked the Wild Child Scraped Face look.

She bent over the sink and touched the scabs.

Ah heck, what was she thinking? Zed made her toes curl. She was a six on a good day, and this sure as heck wasn't a good day. Rick had been a six.

Zed was what, six-foot-five? That automatically made him a six didn't it? Then with those eyes, and that smile? Yeah, he was a ten.

Marcia sat down on the toilet seat. She couldn't do this.

* * *

Zed had heard Marcia running down the hallway. He'd figured she was on her way to dinner, but then…nothing. Time for reconnaissance. The bathroom door was ajar. He could still smell the eucalyptus, cinnamon, and jasmine in the air.

He knocked on the doorjamb. "Marcia?"

"Present," she sounded sad. Her voice was usually lit with music.

"Can I come in?"

"It's your bathroom." Dejected. She sounded dejected.

What was his problem? There she was, slouched over, obviously upset about something, and he immediately notices her red bra strap.

Then she caught him, their eyes held. He pointed at the red lace.

"Is that for me?"

She blushed. "Maybe."

"It goes with the wine I chose."

"Guess there was a hundred percent chance of that, huh?"

He crouched down in front of her and pushed her hair behind her ear. It coaxed her to look him in the eye.

"Wanna tell me what's going on?"

"Not really."

"Want me to guess?" He watched as she truly considered his question.

"I don't like playing those types of games. They're a waste of time. Let's just say I'm having a bit of a pity party and leave it at that, shall we?"

He considered her words. Damn, she was a breath of fresh air. She just spoke her mind, and if she needed a timeout, she wasn't afraid to say so. He loved it. And he was damn close to falling in love with her.

"If I were to say that along with the wine and a medium steak, there was a baked potato with butter, sour cream, chives, cheese, and bacon would that help you out of your funk?" She sat up straighter.

"Bacon bits out of a jar?"

"I cooked the bacon in a frying pan."

"You're in my way." She pushed at his shoulders. "It's dinner time."

He was pretty sure she was faking some of her enthusiasm, but hopefully, by the end of dinner, he will have chased away the clouds in her eyes.

CHAPTER ELEVEN

Marcia was tucked safely away at the shooting range with Wyatt Leeds. Couldn't get much safer than that. Zed looked around the table at the little Mexican taqueria at some of his Black Dawn team mates. Each man had a huge combo platter in front of him, except for Dalton Sullivan, he was always eating healthy. Dalton managed to find a vegetarian burrito. Aiden O'Malley eyed him with disgust, Dalton just raised an eyebrow.

"What's the plan?" Dex Evans asked.

"Easy, kill Felix Raymond. Done deal," Aiden said.

Dex and Aiden bumped fists. Then both sighed and looked at Zed.

"Are we done now?" Zed asked.

"Yeah, it's never that easy," Aiden said.

"What do you mean?" Zed asked.

"Long story."

Hunter sat down with a huge plate. "What'd I miss?"

"Aiden was being a smart-ass about killing Raymond," Zed said in an annoyed tone.

"Yeah, it's never that easy," Hunter said as he took a big bite of his enchilada.

"Shit's going to go wrong, then as soon as you think it's done, it's going to go *really* sideways," Aiden said grimly. "I hate this. I really do. Dealing with our women's lives is worse than a mission."

Zed eyed Aiden and realized he was really upset.

"We're here to make sure nothing more happens to Marcia. Jesus, a python? A fucking *python*?" Dex said, his eyes wide as he stabbed his food. "I've been working the computer with Kane ever since you left for Virginia. Your future father-in-law is into a lot of shit."

Zed put down his soda and stared at Dex. He didn't correct him. He just pondered his statement, amazed Dex had assumed he would be marrying Marcia, like it was a done deal.

"I've been doing more research on Raymond's time here at BUD/S. One of the girls I used to date was a friend of the woman Raymond murdered. She gave me some great insight on how he thinks. It helps to explain why he's targeted your woman," Dalton said.

Zed needed some intel of his own, and Aiden seemed the angriest. "I know you said it was a long story, but how did everything go wrong with Evie?"

Aiden growled. The man literally growled. Hunter's lips twitched upwards.

"Now you've done it," Hunter said.

Aiden shoved his plate away and rested his forearms on the table. He leaned forward and shot Zed a deadly glare. "You feeling a little boxed in Zaragoza? You feeling like we're making some assumptions on your love life?"

Aiden was the only one in the group who was his age. Evie was more than ten years younger than he was. They had some things in common. Some. So Zed was willing to lay some of his cards on the table.

"Yes, hearing Marcia's surrogate father referred to as my father-in-law is a bit disconcerting."

"Love how you throw those four-dollar words around, Zed," Hunter grinned at him. "You and Aiden will end up being BFFs for sure."

"Well, Zed, there's a reason for that," Aiden drawled. "We're just trying to save you some steps. If your head isn't totally in the game right from the start, you might fuck things up and make a wrong move. You do that, and Marcia could be in more danger than she should be. So, just know, you're hooked. Know things are going to get worse before they're going to get better. Know this is going to be a fucked-up op, but we'll have your back."

Zed picked up his drink and took a sip of his limeade. "You were going to tell me about your time with Evie," he prompted.

"I fucked up, and she ran away to Turkey. Ended up being kidnapped and tortured. Then the bastards followed her home to Tennessee, held her sisters hostage, Evie had to kill one of them with a baseball bat. Just when we think it's over, another two of her sisters and her two-year-old niece are almost killed with a bomb." The words were delivered smoothly, but Zed could feel the rage beneath the surface. Aiden O'Malley would never forget or forgive his part in those events.

Zed nodded. He got it. He looked around the table. "Okay, Dalton, let's hear your info first, then Dex, I want to hear what you and Virginia's boy wonder have come up with."

Aiden pulled his plate back in front of him.

* * *

He watched as Wyatt walked Marcia over to his jeep. Even in sneakers, she had a soft seductive sway to her walk. Zed wasn't the only man checking her out, and he wasn't surprised. When she saw him, her hand lifted, and she walked faster across the gravel parking lot.

Wyatt gave him a quick nod as soon as he knew Zed was within touching distance of Marcia.

"Marcia, it was fun, we'll have to do it again sometime," Wyatt smiled at her.

"Absolutely," she smiled at him.

Zed watched as the young SEAL walked away.

Marcia turned to him. "Hello, handsome," she said as he held open the passenger door. After he started the vehicle she turned to him. "You know, you don't have to always do that."

"Do what?"

"Open the passenger door."

"I wouldn't do it if I didn't want to." Zed looked, pulled onto the highway, then glanced over at Marcia. She was biting her lower lip.

"Did you have a good time with Wyatt?"

"He's really good, and he's a great teacher."

"I'll take that as a yes," Zed smiled.

She started to fiddle with the air conditioning, but ultimately, she didn't make any changes. She was nervous. Zed reached over and took her hand and placed it on his thigh, covering it with his. She relaxed back into her seat and started to brush her thumb against his denim covered leg. She was going to kill him, and she wasn't even aware of it.

"What's going on?" he asked.

"I tried to get ahold of Nurul. I couldn't. Do you think you could ask Dex or Kane to help? I'm trying to send some money to her."

"Sure Honey, of course, why didn't you say something sooner?"

"I knew you were busy trying to take over the world. I didn't want to bother you."

"It's not a bother. Never think that." She looked over and gave a soft smile.

"Thanks. Okay, tell me what did you do today?"

"I met with four of the men from Black Dawn."

"Do you like them?"

He shot her a quick glance. "Of course I do, why do you ask?"

"Well," she said softly. "Maybe that's the wrong question. Your normal team in Virginia is Night Storm, you've been with them for five years, right?"

Zed nodded.

"I just wondered if you like and trust these guys the same way you trust your usual team."

"I've been on two missions with this team now. They are first-rate."

He could see her frowning out of the corner of his eye. "What?"

"First-rate sounds like faint praise. What about fantastic? Awesome? Stupendous?"

"I can tell you live with young girls," he teased. "First-rate and First-class are extremely high praise."

"Is that what you'd say about Night Storm?"

"No, I'd call them Fucking First-rate."

"See!"

"Marcia, I was trying to cut down on the swearing for you. Black Dawn is also Fucking First-rate. If they weren't, there isn't a chance in hell I'd be entrusting them with your safety." He picked up her hand and kissed her fingertips. She started to breathe faster. Deeper. Zed realized he wasn't doing much better. He thought about her questions. Black Dawn was fucking first-rate. He thought of Hunter. Their bond was…

Then there was Dex, he would rank him right up there with Kane McNamara. But Night Storm was his home. He was second-in-command, and those men depended on him. Considering everything, Zed had to admit, after today's conversation, Black Dawn was definitely turning into a second home for him.

Ten more minutes and they'd be back at the apartment. This time, he twined his fingers with hers and rested them on her thigh. She closed her eyes and sighed. He concentrated on the drive and getting them home safely. When he parked underneath the covered parking, she opened her door and hopped out before he had a chance to stop her. He put his arm around her and guided her down the path into the complex and unlocked the door, ushering her into the cool living room.

"Marcia, I asked you to let me open your car door," he said pointedly.

"I know, but I'm more than capable. You don't have to do the gentleman thing with me." She meandered over to the kitchen counter and grabbed an apple out of the bowl and took a bite.

He tried to get a read on her and failed. "Two things. I told you I like opening car doors for you. Just like you, I don't play games." He watched her absorb his words, but she didn't seem to take comfort from them. She set the apple down on a paper towel and went to the fridge to pull out a bottle of water. He prowled behind her, and when she turned around, she found herself effectively trapped.

"Number two. I'm opening your car door for your safety."

Her brow wrinkled. "I don't get it."

"I wasn't kidding when I said I wanted to be by your side at all times. This is a safety issue, and I take this very seriously."

"Zed," she smiled. "Come on, nobody's going to do anything with you right there."

He pulled the bottle from her hands and placed it on the counter. Carefully, because for the rest of his life he intended to treat this woman with care, he tilted her chin up so they were eye to eye. "If this were Christie or Debbie, would you be so cavalier?"

Her eyes darkened.

"If Christie and Debbie were standing here, their faces still healing after a kidnapping attempt at the local fucking *mall,*" he gritted out, "tell me Marcia, would you allow them to get out of the car without me right beside them?"

She sucked in a deep breath and shook her head.

"Right answer."

"But seriously, you don't have to with me. I mean, I understand with the car doors, when we're out in the open, but you *always* do it like ushering me into your house. You put your hand on the small of my back and stuff."

"Yes I do," he acknowledged. He watched her, waited for her to explain why that made her uncomfortable.

"I'm not breakable. I'm more than capable of opening my own doors. I don't need this false courtesy."

"False?" His eyebrows raised. "What do you mean false?"

"Nobody does that. They don't mean it. Just be normal."

Even though deep down he was expecting something like this, it still floored him. But he didn't show it, instead he stroked her hair back from her face.

"Can you look at me?"

It took her a moment, but she finally did. "What?"

"Who let you down?"

"Nobody," she said too quickly.

"Who let you down?" he asked again.

"It doesn't matter. I just don't want you to do something that isn't real. I can take care of myself. I don't want to expect something, and it just be taken away," she sounded so sad.

"Think back to the very first moment we met. Have I let you down?"

She frowned. "Well, no."

"I don't intend to and do you know why?"

She shook her head.

"Because you matter to me. You matter one hell of a lot. You can trust me."

She sucked in a deep breath and didn't let it out. He stroked her throat.

"Breathe Baby." She let out a breath. "Will you let me take care of you? Please?"

It was one of the longest moments of his life. Then she nodded.

He dipped his head and captured her lips with his. He was careful all right. Careful to make sure she was on the same page as he was. Careful to ensure when his tongue stroked and plundered, she was eager for him to continue. Last night, he'd taken note of her insecurities and they'd broken his heart. His Marcia should never think she was anything but beautiful and wanted. Zed knew his fingertips were rough and calloused, so he traced the contours of her cheek with a barely there touch, wanting to make sure he was providing pleasure.

Unlike the kiss in Marcia's bedroom back in Virginia, she was tentative. Her hands landed softly on his chest, then in slow increments, crept upwards until she circled his shoulders. Zed continued to stroke her cheek as his other arm brought her body into the curve of his. He needed her close like he needed his next breath.

Marcia moaned into his mouth as she undulated against him. He'd never tasted anything as sweet. Sharp nails bit into the back of his neck, and she wrenched her mouth away from his. He looked into her flushed face.

"Zed," she sighed. Marcia turned her head then shoved it against his neck. Had he done something wrong? He heard her take a deep breath. "You smell so good." He jolted at the feel of her tongue licking his collar bone.

He tried to pull her away, tried to see her eyes, but she wouldn't allow it.

"*Querida*."

"No. Let me. I need to feel you." She kissed his healing scar. "I almost lost you. Before I ever really knew you, I almost lost you."

He had to brace his legs, so he could remain standing. Just thinking of that moment when Kane called him to tell him Marcia was in the hospital. That she had been a victim of an attempted kidnapping. In that moment, he knew Marcia was his future, his love, his life, his everything.

"I want you," he said point-blank.

She swallowed. "I smell like gunpowder."

"No, you smell like jasmine and Marcia. It's been years since I've had to work so hard to control my body's reaction to a woman. You walk into a room and I'm rock-hard."

"Really," he laughed when he saw her shocked expression, "you had no idea?"

She shook her head. "But I hoped."

"You have a lot to make up for. Especially those red panties you took so long to fold."

She looked up at him through a thick fringe of eyelashes, her pink swollen lips tipped into a sly smile. "How do you propose I make it up to you?"

There were so many facets to Marcia, it would take a lifetime to explore. It was going to be so much fun. Zed swooped her up into his arms, and she let out a whoop.

"What the heck do you think you're doing, Mr. Dante Zaragoza?" she asked primly.

So fucking fun, he grinned as he strode into his bedroom. He gently placed her onto the bed.

"You make your bed?"

"You should try it," Zed tried to keep his voice light and teasing, but it came out rough and territorial. Seeing her in his bed did something to him on a primal level. It was like something in him had finally been unlocked.

Marcia held out her arms. She was wearing ripped jeans, sneakers, and a purple peasant blouse. He'd thought she'd looked like a gypsy all day.

"You're looking at me funny," she said tremulously.

"You're beautiful."

Her fingers went up to touch her face. He knelt down on the bed, gripped her wrist, and pulled her hand away.

"Marcia listen to me, you're beautiful. I know this is important to you, so yes, you are healing, but I need you to know, even if the scarring were permanent, you'd still be beautiful."

He watched as her eyes welled with tears. As two escaped he kissed them away. Even her tears tasted good. He lifted up and looked at her.

"I need to know we're on the same page, you want this, right?"

"With everything in me," she choked out.

* * *

Marcia watched wide-eyed as Zed slipped back off the bed and knelt at the bottom. He unlaced her shoes and took them off along with her socks. She heard his indrawn breath as he pushed up her jeans leg to view her calf. He traced the scar. Up and down. Then he bent and traced the red raised flesh with his tongue.

"Does this hurt?"

She had trouble catching her breath, when she finally did, she eked out the word, "No."

"That doesn't sound very sure."

She sat up on her elbows. "Well for goodness sakes, you're caressing me and driving me out of my mind," she said with exasperation.

"I think we can do better than this," he said wickedly. He pulled on her arms, and she was sitting up on the edge of the bed staring into his eyes. "I love this top, but it has to go."

Her mouth went dry. If he was going to take off her blouse that meant she'd get to see what was under his T-shirt. He'd changed clothes once in the jungle, but too much had been going on to truly appreciate it. But right now? Oh, yeah. Without thinking about it, her hands went to the hem of his shirt, and she was drawing it upwards. Zed's eyelids got heavy as he stared at her, but he wasn't stopping her. Marcia continued.

"Lift up your arms," she whispered into the quiet of the room. He did. Once again her eyes were drawn to the pinkened gunshot wound on his neck and upper shoulder. Zed must have figured out the reason for her hesitancy because he threw off his shirt and cupped her face.

"I'm fine Marcia. I'm fine."

She opened her mouth to make a smart-aleck comment about just how fine he was, but she couldn't. He could have died. Too many people in her life had died. Then she slowly realized, that was exactly the point, and she smiled. Darn it, this moment in time was important, it was glorious, it was meant to be savored.

She spread her palms against his warm chest, loving the feel of all that heat and power. She was so entranced, she didn't realize Zed was untucking her blouse from her jeans until he told her to lift up her arms. Reluctantly, she did.

"I was hoping you were wearing the lavender bra," he confided.

She barely heard him, all of her concentration focused on getting her hands back on his chest. The man even had an eight-pack. Marcia stroked her hands down his ridged abdomen, and she sighed in pleasure.

"Ahhh," he groaned. He liked. Well then, how about this? She grinned when he moaned as she scraped her nails up the center of his body.

Marcia had been concentrating so hard on his responses, she was shocked when Zed's warm hands encased her bare breasts.

"I love front opening bras," he murmured. She whimpered when his thumbs stroked her swollen nipples. "Again. I love the sounds you make." Marcia pushed up against his palms.

Fire raced through her, she had never experienced anything close to this level of desire before. Why? Was it Zed? Was it because she'd been so close to death?

"I must be doing this wrong," Zed said. His thumbs started to circle the tight nubs of flesh.

"Huh?"

"You're thinking too hard."

How'd he know she'd been questioning…?

"Oh, no," she let out a shrill cry as his mouth encompassed one swollen nipple. His tongue swirled, round and round, her other nipple pinched in a matching rhythm.

Were those sounds coming from her?

Marcia loved the feel of his rough silk hair. He did something that drove her wild, and she yanked at his hair and relished the groan that vibrated against her taut flesh. He suckled her harder. She was panting so hard, trying to take in air, she thought she might pass out.

Zed's head lifted. "Easy, *Querida*, we have all night."

Huh? This couldn't go on that long. She could only handle this for five more minutes!

"Let's get you out of these jeans, shall we?" His fingers were already working on the button of her jeans. She so wanted this, but it was so much more than she ever imagined. How could her jeans be off? He was a magician. She grabbed at her purple panties, and he looked up at her giving her a considering look.

"You want to torture me, don't you?" She'd never heard his voice so deep.

She nodded, then shook her head.

"Ah, Baby, you don't have to be shy. I'll take care of you."

Wait a darn minute! Her spine straightened.

"I'm not a child. I have had sex before. Maybe it's me who's going to take care of you!"

His thumb whispered across her bottom lip as his hot gaze looked her over.

"I would never mistake you for a child, *Querida*. I meant no offense. We are definitely equals, and we always will be. How about we take turns, sometimes, you take care of me, and sometimes, I take care of you?"

She searched his face. She saw nothing but sincerity. And in truth, today she would love to have him take the lead. "I would like that." Then she replayed his words. "Always?" she questioned.

"One day at a time," he soothed. "Right now, I want to investigate these panties," he smiled tenderly. He traced the lace at the top, then he coaxed her legs to widen, so he could examine the lace along the lower edge. "So pretty, so soft." She didn't think he was talking about the purple silk as he traced the panel.

Zed took his time peeling them off her body, and she did nothing but hold her breath. Slowly he spread her legs, and she watched in fascination as he stared at the very heart of her.

"You're beautiful." She blushed.

His thumbs parted her intimate flesh. "You're so wet for me."

For a moment she came out of stupor. "What would you expect, you're sex-on-a-stick."

He threw back his head and laughed. "Marcia, I am so thankful this is a two way street. I would be heartbroken if we didn't share this passion."

He would? Then his thumb moved and touched her exactly right, the nub of flesh that drove her crazy. She felt his warm breath, her only warning before his tongue touched her.

"Zed," she cried out. Slowly, softly, he caressed her. Again and again, his tender ministrations drove her up and up into a whole other plane of existence. All she could say was his name, over and over again. He was the center of her universe.

"Now," he whispered.

With his command, she hurled into space.

* * *

Zed sat back, his heart racing. He traced her trembling thighs, trying to calm down, so he would be able to make love to Marcia and make it last. He'd never been blessed with a more responsive lover in his life. When he thought he had a modicum of control, he got up and stripped out of his jeans. He went to his nightstand and took out his unopened box of condoms.

Zed turned to look at Marcia who was now watching him with a dazed look on her face. He pulled one out, and put a knee on the bed, then stole a slow kiss from the woman who was his world. Her arms twined around his neck, and if there was any discomfort, he didn't notice it. Another kiss. He needed another kiss. He peppered her face with kisses.

"Please Zed, I need you."

He moved her to the middle of the bed, then stroked his hand down the center of her body until once again he found her heat. She arched up, and he tested her depths. One finger. God, she felt so good, two fingers. He stroked her, and she sighed. He continued to caress her until she gasped her pleasure.

"What?" she asked tremulously. "What are you doing?"

"Making you feel good."

Shit, he was going to lose it. Come on, thirty-six. You're thirty-six, get it together Zaragoza.

He pulled out his fingers and licked them, then rolled on the condom.

"Please, now. Now."

He positioned himself at her opening. He knew he needed to go slowly, she was so tight.

"Just do it," she said fiercely.

Nothing could have slowed him down more than those words. He searched her face and realized his beautiful Marcia didn't know the first thing about making love. "Shhh, we'll get there."

He pressed in slowly, just a little. She gave a soft cry, her smile told him that it was pleasure.

"More."

He kept himself up on his elbows and gave her more. With every thrust, she smiled brighter until he was fully sheathed.

"So good," she sighed. "We're together, it's so good."

She bowed her body upwards and captured his mouth in a kiss. He started a rhythm as old as time. Marcia cupped his cheeks as her beautiful legs wrapped around his waist drawing him closer.

He felt her body shudder and tighten. Thank fuck, he wasn't going to last. She tore her mouth from his.

"Zed," she whimpered. He saw tears filling her eyes. "Oh Zed," she cried out as her body clamped around him, her nails scoring his back. "So perfect. So perfect," she sobbed, and he catapulted into bliss.

CHAPTER TWELVE

She woke to the smell of oranges. Marcia rolled over and saw Zed placing a tray on the bedside table. Her eyes widened when she saw everything that was on it.

"Are we expecting company?" she asked as she scooted up against the headboard, holding the sheet over her breasts.

"I don't share." Marcia blushed as his gaze raked over her. Before she had a chance to feel uncomfortable, a slow smile broke crossed his face, and she relaxed. "Hungry?" he asked.

She nodded. Zed sat down on the bed beside her and brought the tray between them.

"I stepped out while you were asleep."

She reached for a piece of cheese and a cracker, but her heart turned over when she saw the strawberries and bowl of chocolate sauce.

"You're a romantic," she whispered.

"I have my moments."

"And you're okay with eating crackers in bed? I would have thought that went against the whole Navy man mentality."

Zed handed her a glass of wine. "There are always exceptions, otherwise life isn't worth living," he smiled. "Don't you need two hands to eat?"

Marcia looked down and realized her left hand was clutching the sheet like it was a lifeline. She licked her lips and released the sheet. Slowly, it slid down, then caught on the swell of her breasts. She watched in fascination as Zed's eyes gleamed; it gave her a wicked thrill. When the fabric pooled into her lap, she no longer felt exposed, instead, she felt liberated.

Zed swirled a strawberry in the bowl of chocolate, then held it up to her lips. She bit into the sweet fruit, the flavor bursting across her tongue.

"You're gorgeous."

Marcia couldn't think of anything to say in response, so she took another bite. It was as if Zed understood. When she was done, he handed her back her glass of wine.

"Would you tell me about Rick?" he asked.

"If you'll tell me more about what it was like growing up in LA," she countered.

"Deal."

"I was stupid. I should have been able to see through him."

"What do you mean?"

"He always said what I wanted to hear. He pretended like I mattered. He listened to what I had to say like it was important. I should have been able to see he was too good to be true." Marcia looked around, then set down her glass of wine on the night stand and started to grab the sheet. Zed took her hand in his.

"Honey, how were you supposed to be able to see he was bullshitting you?"

"Because nobody's really like that."

He watched her carefully as she pulled up the sheet with her other hand.

"How long were you and Rick together?"

"A little over two years. I thought. I thought…"

He gave her hand a gentle squeeze. "What did you think, Marcia?"

"I thought we were going to get married." It took everything she had to hold back a sob. Why was she being so emotional about something that was done and dust? Somehow, the tray was on the floor and her head was resting on Zed's shoulder, the sheet over both of them. He was stroking his fingers over her shoulder. Her breathing was getting back to normal. At least she hadn't done a full-on cry. What an idiot.

"Be nice to my woman," he whispered into her hair.

"What do you mean?"

"You're too hard on yourself. Everybody else in your life, you will bend over backwards for and do everything in the world to make sure they get a soft spot to land, but you are amazingly hard on yourself."

"Don't be nice to me," she mumbled into his chest.

He tilted her chin up to meet her eyes. "Marcia, let's get one thing straight, I'm not Rick. I'm not pretending to be nice to you."

"You're nothing at all like him, I know that. It's just…"

"Just what?"

"I'm scared. I want you too much. I need you too much. You're already a thousand times more important than Rick ever was to me, and if he couldn't really love me, how can you?"

He pulled her even closer. "You're kidding, right?" he rumbled.

* * *

Marcia's skin was chilled, so Zed stroked her bare arms with his hands, trying to warm her. Her sherry brown eyes looked up at him expectantly. What should he tell her? The truth? Should he tell her when he first saw her photo, he knew they were destined to have a future together? What would she think of him if she knew he had those kinds of premonitions? He decided to go with something that was true, just not the full truth.

"Marcia, from the first moment I saw you, I knew you were going to be someone special in my life." She tried to pull away, but he wouldn't let her. "Without my instincts I wouldn't be alive today, they have pulled me through ten years of special operations, and those instincts were very much spot on when they told me what a remarkable woman you are."

He watched her consider his words. He could see her entire process, it was one of the things he loved about her, she truly didn't have a poker face. First, there was the fury he would lie to her, then the hurt, then he saw her wheels turn even further.

"Zed, you're not the type of man to lie, but you're wrong," she said slowly.

"What am I wrong about?"

"I'm not remarkable."

He cupped the back of her head and brought her forehead to rest against his.

"So, says the woman who adopts a young mother and a baby in the jungle, fights a python, and babysits the nations NSA Director. Sure, there's nothing remarkable about you."

Zed saw her eyes widen. "Well when you put it like that," she drawled. "Maybe you should like me a little bit."

"Let's not forget the part where you are dynamite in bed," he reminded her.

He had never in his life seen someone blush from the tips of their hairline down to the tops of their breasts before. Lord have mercy.

"And you got one thing wrong in that statement, Querida," he said as his fingers traced her blush.

"What?" she asked breathlessly. Her eyes were staring at him as her body shivered under his touch.

"I don't just like you, I love you with all of my heart."

Two tears dripped down her face, and once again, Zed was tortured with the view of her even, white teeth torturing her bottom lip. She searched his face, and he waited. He didn't know what she was looking for, but she must have found it. Marcia's fingers fluttered over his neck before landing on his cheek.

"I'm in love with you too," she whispered.

Zed felt a part of himself relax, a part of his soul that had been guarded and restless for decades was fulfilled by her words. "Thank fucking God," he said, right before he claimed her mouth.

* * *

Zed opened one eye and pretended to scowl. Marcia giggled as she wiped up the drizzled chocolate sauce on his chest with the strawberry. She'd been giving him a hard time about cleanliness in the bed for the last four hours, thinking he would mind her shenanigans. She was wrong on all counts. As long as she was naked in his bed, he was a happy man.

He was really happy to see that for the last four hours, she had been totally unselfconscious about her appearance. Even after the first chocolate shower they'd shared, she hadn't given a second look at her face, instead, she'd been more interested in his shaving routine.

"You do realize we're going to have to shower again?" he asked.

Marcia popped the chocolate covered strawberry into his mouth, and he chewed.

"I bet I can make you not care," she purred.

He bet she was right.

"You still haven't stuck to your part of the bargain," she said as she licked delicately at a drop of chocolate on his chest.

What was she talking about?

"Hmmm?" he asked.

"You were going to tell me about growing up in East LA."

Looking at Marcia's wealth of tumbling curls and thinking about her huge heart, he couldn't help but smile. "My abuela would have loved you."

"That's grandmother, right?"

"Yes. She had my mother when she was fifteen, then my mother had me when she was sixteen. They looked more like sisters than mother and daughter."

She stopped moving, her eyes overly bright. "Oh Zed, you're talking about them in the past tense."

"They've both passed," he nodded. "It's been years and years."

She didn't ask any questions, she just got out of bed, went to the master bath, and came back with a warm wash cloth, wiping the chocolate off his chest, then cuddled up next to him.

"When I was really little, we lived in a small apartment, and I remember a lot of laughter. Actually, a lot of singing too. And the food. My grandmother was a great cook. My mom? Not so much."

"The arguing started when I was about six. Mom would leave for days on end, and when she would come back, she wasn't the mom I remembered. Later, I realize she was either high or strung out, but to the eyes of a six-year-old, those rages just seemed like your mom all of a sudden hated you."

Marcia's hand clenched over his chest. She knew what it was like dealing with an addict. "What did your grandmother do?"

"Mom started to bring men back to the apartment. When my grandmother was at work, one of them knocked me across the room, then locked me outside. She found me on the porch. I'd never seen my *Abuela* so angry. She took me to a neighbor's apartment and had me spend the night. I never saw my mother again, it was a couple of years later that she died."

"I'm so sorry," Marcia said. He could hear the ache in her voice.

"My *Abuela's* name was Carmalita Margaurite Zaragoza, quite a mouthful, huh?"

"Zaragoza?"

"Yeah, mom was illegitimate, and so was I. Abuela would tell me stories about her family from Mexico." His lips twitched. "When I went to school and started hearing fairy tales, I realized she had pretended fairy tales were really stories about her family. I never called her on it because by then, I was seven or eight years old and realized telling me those stories and having me believe good things about her family back in Mexico made her happy."

"She sounds wonderful. What happened to her?"

"She died of cancer. I just thank God it happened after I pulled my head out of my ass." Marcia's head shot off his chest at the vehemence in his words.

"What do you mean?"

"Abuela worked as a seamstress. It paid better than housekeeping, and she made sure we had enough to more than get by. In my old neighborhood that meant she was able to take us from an apartment to renting a house, so we weren't in the thick of the gang territory when I was nine years old. Don't get me wrong, at the school I was in, we were surrounded, but I was a big kid for my age, I didn't have to be pulled in like some kids."

Zed thought back to the summer he joined *Las Nuevas Espadas*. They'd been trying to recruit him for over a year. He'd been fourteen. All he was going to do was a few small things, just enough to spend time with some of his friends who were part of the gang and have money saved for a kickass car when he turned sixteen. He wouldn't cross any hard lines. He justified everything. By the time he had his money, he'd have already quit, and Abuela would be none the wiser.

He unlocked the door to the little house. He didn't smell any food cooking.

"Abuelita?" Zed called out. The little house was dark, all the drapes were pulled, blocking out the California sun.

"I'm home," he hollered out again. His grandmother's car had been in the tiny little drive beside the house. Where was she? Zed

flung his backpack on the couch and went to the kitchen. He was hungry. Maybe there were some leftovers in the fridge.

He found some foil wrapped tamales. He grabbed those as well as an orange soda.

"What?!" He almost dropped everything on the floor when he turned to find his small little grandmother standing in front of him. She was dressed entirely in black with a black shawl over her head.

"Abuelita? What's wrong? Who died?" He dumped the food and drink down on the counter and pulled her trembling hand in his and walked her over to the small kitchen table. "Talk to me. What's wrong?" Zed had only seen her dressed like this when they had attended Mr. Fuentes funeral.

"You know what is wrong, Dante," his grandmother said in Spanish. She never called him Dante. He noted the rosary beads in her hands. It was at that moment, he knew, somehow, she knew. She had found out about his meeting with Red Blade, the leader of Las Nuevas Espadas.

How could she have found out about something that had just happened three hours ago? He looked at her, astounded.

"Are you going to try to lie?"

Yes. Hell, yes, he was going to lie. Zed looked wildly around the kitchen, anyplace except at the woman who had raised him. The woman who somehow knew *things. He was so fucked.*

"I don't know what you're talking about. You're talking crazy," he said.

She gave a slow regal nod, almost as if she'd been expecting those very words.

"You are still a child, Dante. You may live under my roof. Do not let your new ways taint this house. You have until the day you are eighteen before your decision will make you dead to me. You know better than this."

He looked at her, trying to grasp her words. "Abuelita," he started.

"Since I was never married, the proper form of address is Señorita Zaragoza," she said as she stood up. "Do not leave this until it is too late, Dante."

It was on the tip of his young, smart-ass tongue to tell her to call him Señor Zaragoza.

"I would advise against it," she said as she swept out of the room.

Zed dropped down onto the kitchen chair she had just vacated and picked up the rosary beads, then dropped them back down on the table. He sat straight up.

Dammit, he was old enough to think for himself. He knew what he was doing.

Zed looked down at Marcia whose eyes were wide.

"How did she know? Had someone told her?"

"Not often, but occasionally, the Zaragoza's would know things. I remember once, there was a little girl who came to our house with her dad, asking if we had seen her dog. My grandmother told her her dog was over at the animal shelter across the city. The man just laughed. Two days later they came back and thanked my grandmother because that's where they found the little girl's dog. I asked my grandmother how she knew. She just shrugged her shoulders and said sometimes, she just knew things."

Zed waited to see how Marcia would respond to that. He'd only told four people that story in his entire life, Marcia now made five. She kissed his shoulder and smiled.

"You can do that too, can't you?"

He didn't answer directly. "Why do you say that?"

"I like numbers. I mean I *really* like numbers," Marcia's eyes twinkled.

"Okay. I have absolutely no idea where this is going."

"Occasionally, when I'm looking at something, a really complex problem, I know the answer. I mean a problem that's going to take me four hours of calculations to come up with the answer, but I know what the answer is. All my calculations are going to do is just confirm what I already know. It's weird, Zed. It's spooky and otherworldly and even though we just talked about loving one another?"

He started to smile and nodded.

"So, even though I love you?" she said in a voice barely above a whisper. "I don't know that I ever would have admitted the whole math voodoo to you if I didn't know you have voodoo, too."

Zed burst out laughing and rolled her over, so he was looking down at her.

"I love you, Marcia Price."

"Tell me how you pulled your head out of your ass. Did you do it before you were eighteen?"

"I'd moved out by the time I was sixteen," Zed shook his head. "I was a lot smarter than she was, just ask me. I did a lot of stuff I'm not proud of, but there were lines I never crossed. I thought I had gotten away with it because there had been so many turf wars going on. I thought I had slipped through the cracks. I thought I was smart, but I was so fucking stupid." Zed rolled onto his back and stared up at the ceiling. Wisdom came at a high price.

"What happened?"

"Because there had been so many little turf wars that had come along, I had skated along without having to kill anyone."

"Kill anyone?" she breathed out. "You were a kid."

"I was in a notorious gang, and I was a punk. When Luis gave me the gun and told me what I needed to do, he made it sound like I would be doing the world a favor by getting rid of this guy. To this day, I regret I considered it, just so I could stay part of something I knew was wrong. But Luis had also made it clear if I didn't do it, not only would I die, but so would my family."

When Marcia whimpered, he pulled her close and pressed a kiss to her temple.

"How d'you get out of it and protect your grandmother?"

He squeezed his eyes shut, then grinned down at her.

"That's a lot of faith you have in an eighteen-and-a-half-year-old screw up."

"Zed, I've seen you in action."

"Luis was supposed to watch it go down. I was supposed to tell him the time and location of the drive-by, so he could report back." Zed sighed. "I set him up. I tipped off the other gang, and they were waiting for Luis and his men. It all spiraled out of control for two weeks."

"What about your grandmother?"

"With all the crazy going on, we had a week to get her packed up to visit relatives down in Guadalajara. By the time I got to her house, she had a telephone number of a Navy recruitment officer."

Zed kept that piece of paper in the same frame as the picture he had of Señorita Zaragoza. Marcia's fingertips teasing through his hair brought his focus back to her.

"When did she pass?"

"Two weeks after I received my trident," Zed smiled. He just wished she could have been alive to have met Marcia.

CHAPTER THIRTEEN

"I won't be put off by fantastic sex again. As a matter of fact, it is off the table until you tell me what the hell is going on!" Gah! Couldn't the man even look slightly unsettled when she yelled at him?

Zed looked up from his laptop, then closed it.

"Good to know it's fantastic sex." He reached out a hand, and she slapped it away.

"Absolutely not, buster. You got out of bed in the middle of the night, and I hear you out here talking to Kane, but you haven't been keeping me informed of what's going on. I don't like it one bit."

She wasn't going to admit to him for just a moment or two she thought of Rick and had a momentary flashback when she'd heard Zed out here in the living room talking to his friend on a computer call. So, start with insecurity, then find out they'd been getting information on Jefferies, and Zed had been keeping her in the dark, and now, she was ready to spit nails.

"Marcia, come sit down next to me." He held out his hand again. It was so tempting. Seeing Zed there, in his bronze gloriousness, wearing nothing but boxers was tough to resist, but she was going to. It was a matter of principal.

"Tell me what's going on," she insisted.

"I will. You don't have to sit next to me. But if you do, I can show you some things on the computer, it's easier this way."

"Oh." She grabbed his hand like she'd wanted to and sat down next to him. "So, what are you going to show me?"

"*Querida*, first I want to say thank you," his voice was so solemn, but his eyes twinkled devilishly.

"Uhmm, okay. I'll bite. For what?"

"For telling Kane we have fantastic sex," he drawled.

"Oh, no," she wailed. "Did he hear me?"

"Oh, yeah," Zed's smile flashed white, "he did."

Suck it up. Just suck it up and stay on point.

"Show me what's on your laptop," she waved her hand to the computer resting on his knees, "and tell me what's going on

Zed was still chuckling when he opened the computer.

"Now Marcia, in all honesty, after my session with Jackson tomorrow, you and I were going to meet with the team to go over things."

She knocked her ankle against his. "I guess I might have gone over the top, huh?"

"You do tend to have a temper." Before she could apologize, he kept talking, "But I happen to love your fiery side."

The man was making her blush again. Would that ever stop happening?

A picture of Raymond filled the laptop, but not as she remembered him. He was wearing Navy dress whites.

"That's just all sorts of wrong," she said.

"I agree," Zed said grimly. "He's gone off the grid, but Harold's brought in an FBI Profiler to try to determine why Raymond became focused on you, and what he hopes to gain."

Marcia laughed and held up her hand like a kid in school. Zed looked at her with that raised eyebrow of his.

"Yes?" he asked.

"I know the answer to this one. He's a misogynist, and I made fun of him and shot him."

"And for extra credit, can you tell me what he hopes to gain?" Zed asked.

"He wants to make me die painfully."

"You have just passed the Navy SEAL profiler class, Ms. Price. Congratulations. However, the correct usage of batshit, crazy motherfucker was not used."

Damn, this man was perfect. Just listening to his laugh, a girl could get lost in those eyes. Stay focused. Focused. But that chest, and those biceps.

"Okay, what about Jefferies?" she asked when her voice wouldn't tremble.

"That man is profit motivated, but it turns out, he's made a new friend who has political motivations. His new friend is a Russian oligarch who has made friends with a new nationalist in Turkey."

"So, Jefferies could be after either of Mr. B's projects for financial gain, but the nuclear materials seem to work better with the new Russian guy."

"That about sums it up."

"So, do you have a plan?"

"I always have plans." Zed shut his computer and set it on the coffee table. "I told you, tomorrow after physical therapy, we're going to meet with the team. But tonight, I think I need to work on some repetitive movements to show Jackson I've made progress."

"Really?" Marcia sighed disgustedly. "You're a thirty-six-year-old Navy man, for God's sake. That's your best line to get sex?"

"Rumor has it, it's fantastic sex."

"Only because of all the effort I put it into it," Marcia said as she flounced off the sofa. The T-shirt she was wearing had ridden up, but why pull it down? Instead, she swayed down the hall and gave herself a mental high five when Zed picked her up and carried her the rest of the way to the bed.

* * *

Zed had the phone to his ear before the first ring finished.

"Zaragoza."

"The Brockman's house was car bombed," Kane said. He looked over at Marcia who was still asleep in the faint dawn light. He got up, shut the bedroom door, then went out to the living room. He turned on his computer with Kane continuing to relay information to him.

"Do we know survivors?" he whispered his question.

"It didn't hit the house, only got as far as that massive front gate, but still, it was a huge payload. Killed the driver and three pedestrians, instantly. I'm not being coy about the family, the front of the house is caved in. I just don't have answers on the family yet. Should know something any minute. Just stay away from the TV. I'll call as soon as I get something."

Zed didn't have to stay away from the TV, he had aerial footage on his laptop.

He had to wake up Marcia.

He went back to the bedroom and pulled on a pair of clean shorts, and grabbed a clean tee and pajama bottoms for Marcia. The Brockman's had to be all right. He didn't know how Marcia could be expected to live with more loss in her life.

He kissed her healed cheek. "Querida?"

She smiled up at him. In an instant, she knew something was wrong.

"Just tell me."

"There's been a bomb. It's still too early to know who's injured or to what extent, but you need to know."

Her eyes had adjusted, and she saw the clothes. Her hands trembled when she reached for them.

"Let me help you."

Marcia nodded. Zed helped to thread her arms through the arm holes, then he held the pajama bottoms in place, so she could step into them, as if she were a child. He wrapped his arms around her, kissing the top of her head. He wanted to tell her it was going to be okay, but what would be the point if in five minutes her world would unravel?

He sat on the side of the bed with her in his lap, the phone on the bed beside them like the snake in the Garden of Eden, waiting to strike. It was supposed to take just minutes, but it felt like an hour Marcia had been trembling in his arms. Had he done the right thing waking her?

The phone rang, and he put it on speaker.

"Kane, it's me and Marcia."

She kept her head pressed into the crook of his neck. Her mouth was open in a wordless scream, just waiting to be set off.

"There are four people, all alive, being loaded onto ambulances. I don't know their condition. Just that all four of them are alive."

Marcia jerked up. "There should be five. Aunt Vi is there too."

"I know," Kane said. "I told them there should be five. Marcia it's a goatfuck there. They haven't even been able to tell me if it's four women or three women and a man, how many of them are kids. Nothing."

"I need to get there," Marcia said, struggling to get out of his arms.

"We don't know if this is a set-up," Kane protested.

"So, fix it that I'm protected," she shouted. "I have to be there."

"No," Kane said.

"Kane," Zed's voice cut through the pre-dawn hours, Marcia's head whipped around to look at him. "Never talk to Marcia like that again unless we are on a mission, and it's life threatening."

"Got it, Zed. I'll start figuring out how to make this work."

"Appreciate it. Work with Dex on this side."

"I planned to. It'll be fun finally getting to wake his ass up at the butt-crack of dawn," Kane laughed. With that joke, Zed knew they were good.

When he disconnected, he focused all of his attention on Marcia.

"You'll be there soon. Even better, Kane will probably be calling back in five minutes with more details."

Her small hands were laying, palms up in her lap. She was staring at the wall. To anyone else, it might look like she was giving up, but Zed could actually feel the energy she was gathering around herself. She was harnessing her resources. She turned to look at him.

"That meeting you were going to have. Can it be now? Can your team come here while Kane gets his information?" She gnawed at her lip. "I mean they have to help set up protection, anyway, right?"

She was right. It was perfect.

He picked up his phone.

* * *

Marcia was at the point where she thought she might throw up. She'd been trying to get ahold of Mr. B., but he wasn't answering, and the uncertainty was killing her. She knew she had to stay strong and focused, but what she really wanted to do was scream and cry. They were waiting on Dex and Gray to show up.

She was trying to rub the kink out of her neck when she heard smoky, soft laughter. She turned and saw Evie O'Malley step out onto the balcony with her.

"Let me guess, your neck hurts because you keep having to look up at all those tall men," Evie said in a Southern drawl.

Marcia nodded. "I couldn't understand why Aiden brought you here to begin with, but now I'm just so grateful to have someone I can look in the eye, I don't care about the why anymore."

"I brought lemonade and sparkling water, take your choice, they're both for you. I figured you probably didn't need any more caffeine this morning."

Marcia took the glass of lemonade and drank a long sip.

"Thank you," she sighed. "So, why are you here?"

"I'm here to tell you that you're not alone. That these men will take care of you. One of my best friends was rescued by a SEAL from a Mexican jungle."

"I don't want to be rescued, I wanted to rescue myself," Marcia said fiercely.

The smaller woman snorted and drank down half the glass of water. "Yeah, well that's how Lydia has felt ever since Clint carried her out of that jungle. Trust me, she kicks ass. She helped me save my sister. I was just trying to say with all this firepower," Evie waved her hand towards the men gathered inside, "plus the girls on your side, we'll take down the fuckers."

"God, I hope so. It's been almost an hour, and they still don't know if it's Vi or Lesley who is missing. How can they not know?" Marcia looked at Evie helplessly.

Both women looked up as Zed opened the sliding glass door.

"Would it hurt you to bend over every once in a while?" Evie muttered.

Zed ignored her as he looked at Marcia. "Harold's on the phone, he wants to talk to you before being put on speaker."

Marcia couldn't feel her legs, they had the substance of water. Zed had his arm around her in a heartbeat. He drew her down to one of the chairs and handed her the phone.

"Marcia?"

"Mr. B.? What's going on?"

"Christie and Debbie are fine."

"What does that mean? Burns? Bruises?"

"Just scared out their minds, but fine. It's because of where their bedrooms are."

"Thank God. Who's missing then? Kane told me only four people were found at the house."

"Lesley's missing. She wasn't home, and I didn't know she'd left the house." He sounded anguished.

"What happened to Vi that she couldn't explain who she was? Are you sure she left voluntarily? Are you okay?" Marcia thought she might drop the phone, she was trembling so badly.

Zed scooched his chair beside her and put his arm around her shoulders.

"Easy," he breathed into her hair.

Marcia slammed the speaker button on the phone, so Zed could hear Mr. B.'s answers.

"Vi was in the living room watching television, and she was knocked out. I was in my study and the bookcase fell and trapped me along with the part of the outside wall that was blown in. By the time they put me in the ambulance, they'd already transported Vi and the two girls. I have some of my former men checking everyplace for Lesley."

"Her phone?" Zed asked.

"I'll have the records in the next ten minutes," Brockman answered. "I'm praying this is nothing more than her normal bad behavior."

"How's Vi now?" Marcia asked.

Brockman gave a weak chuckle. "I think this is old hat for you, honey. Contusions and a concussion."

"I'll be there tonight."

"No!" he sounded almost like Kane had.

"I want to be there for my family."

"And I want, your family wants you with you here with us," Brockman said tiredly. "But NSA and Homeland Security are all over this. It's made international news. What you don't know is Al-Qaeda has taken credit."

"Does that mean it has something to do with Yemen and the Saudis?" Marcia asked.

"ISIS has taken credit too." Marcia could hear the man's exhaustion. He needed her.

"I'll be there—"

"Zaragoza, if you were running this op, what would your decision be?"

"She'd stay here. Too many moving parts in D.C. right now. You have no idea if this is part of your old job, Jefferies, or whatever pies you currently have your hands in. Meanwhile, we know Jefferies and Raymond are threats we have to neutralize, and we've been working some angles on that."

"Do you have any leads?"

"Yeah, we do. We're going to review them with Marcia in a few minutes. Dex or Kane will keep you informed unless you want to be part of the conversation."

"I've got to get back to the girls," Marcia heard Mr. B. sigh. "Meanwhile, you keep my girl Marcia safe, you hear me?"

"I do. And I will." Zed disconnected the phone.

* * *

Zed saw Gray and Dex come into his apartment. Aiden was at the sliding glass door, motioning Evie to come inside. Zed put his arm around Marcia and took her into the living room which seemed exceedingly small, now that it housed so many large men.

"How's your family, Marcia?" Gray asked as she settled onto the couch.

"Physically fine, but Lesley's missing. She just got out of a rehabilitation clinic. She's pulled stunts like this before after her first two in-stays." Zed heard the pain in her voice. He'd really hoped it would be different for Lesley this time on Marcia's behalf. He just thanked God, the other four Brockman's were doing well.

Dalton cleared his throat, and all eyes turned to him. "Marcia, I've got your family in my prayers," he said solemnly. From what Zed knew about the man's past, he knew he was sincere.

"Thank you," Marcia responded.

"I have some information regarding Raymond," Dalton said. Dex handed him a file and Dalton reached in and pulled out a photo he handed to Marcia. She tilted it so Zed could see it. The picture showed Raymond with his arm around a petite blonde woman and another couple at the beach near Dana Point.

"This is Felix Raymond with his girlfriend Layla Martin. She was dead five months after this photo was taken," Dalton said. "I spoke to Renee, she's the girl standing beside Layla, she was Layla's best friend. She had a lot to say about our boy Raymond."

Marcia nodded. Then Dalton handed over another photo.

This time it was of Raymond in a team softball jersey. It showed him getting ready to throw a pitch.

"This is from the co-ed softball team they were all on. Turns out Raymond didn't like to lose. So much so, Renee's boyfriend finally admitted to her the night before a tournament, he and good ole Felix went to talk to the pitcher on the other team. Renee's boyfriend swears he just thought they were going to bribe him to throw the game. Instead, Raymond broke two of his fingers on his right hand, so he couldn't pitch."

"Great, he's a cheater and a bully too," Marcia mumbled.

"Turns out this guy worked at the bank where Raymond had his car loan. He worked with his boss to get it repossessed. Renee said Layla offered to loan him the money for a down payment for a new loan. It was the first time he hit her."

"He hit her for trying to help him?" Wyatt's confusion was obvious as he asked the question.

"His little feelings got hurt because she was in a better financial position," Evie said.

"That was half of it," Dalton agreed.

"Let me guess, he then came back at her and demanded she buy the thing outright for him," Marcia said.

Dalton nodded. "You're right," he agreed sadly.

Zed knew the real reason Dalton was pensive. He looked around the room and saw similar looks on all the men's faces. They didn't like the idea of these two women knowing the intimate working of such an abusive personality. It meant they'd had to learn how to cope, so they could survive. Zed now wondered whether there was any physical abuse in her relationship with Rick.

"How long after that before he killed her?" Marcia asked.

"It was nine weeks," Dalton said softly. "There's more. Renee never thought much of it, but it turned out that Marty, the pitcher from the other team, up and moved stakes soon after the whole car fiasco. Years later, she found out the reason why he'd left; his home had been invaded and his wife had been assaulted."

Zed watched Marcia nod her head like she wasn't surprised. God knows he wasn't. He waited for the next shoe to drop.

The next thing Dalton handed Marcia was a newspaper printout of a bicyclist who had been the victim of a hit and run on Pacific Coast Highway.

"This is our banker friend's boss," Dex said. "Unfortunately, there had been enough hit and runs where bicyclists are concerned, nobody thought to look at this as premeditated."

"None of this came up during the trial?" Marcia asked.

Dalton shook his head.

"But you've got more, don't you?" Marcia looked between Dalton and Dex.

"Yeah, there's more," Dex said. He pulled out three photos from the file and handed them all to Marcia. "These are all men who have died at Thorpe International, two of them stateside. When Kane and I started to make inquiries regarding who Raymond had run-ins with, this pattern emerged."

"Three dead men in eight years, that's all you've been able to confirm, right?" Marcia leaned over and drilled Dexter with a look. "You know there's more."

"Yep, that's what my gut's saying too, but these are damn near certain. So, we've got a serial killer on our hands, and you are his number one target."

Marcia waved her hand like it didn't matter, and Zed gritted his teeth. "Dex, you have more than just five slides. So, we know we have an itty-bitty problem with Raymond, who's up next."

"This isn't a joke," Zed spit out.

She whirled to look at him, and she was going to mouth off something smart-ass, but thank God, she figured out now was not the time.

"Zed, I know it's not a joke," she said quietly as her hand landed on his thigh. "But I also know your team, and especially you, won't let anything happen to me."

"What else do you have?" Zed asked Dex.

This time Dex handed the picture to Zed.

"Solomon Jefferies, former Assistant Director of the NSA." Zed studied the picture of the man Dex handed him. He wanted to see if this time he would discern something new if he looked at it.

"Kane finally found something interesting," Dex said.

"Kane?" Gray said.

"Kane, me, who's keeping score," Dex scoffed. "Anyway, here's the deal. Our man Jefferies' new BFF, Vitoly Akulov, he's a bastard."

Everyone laughed, except for Zed.

"So, this isn't about Jefferies' friends in Turkey, is it? Who's his father?"

Dex shook his head. "His father is the former head of the Republic of Crimea. The one who is currently in exile."

"So, we could potentially have a Crimea with nuclear weapons?" Marcia asked aghast. Then she paused and slowly shook her head. "There's no way Jefferies would allow that much instability to happen. Unless he's a total warmonger. What's his motivation? Money or instability?"

"Since I found out some former members of Thorp group have taken a commission to eliminate Vitoly, I'm going to have to say Jefferies was in it for the money, but now, he's doing what he can to mitigate things. He would be looking for a new buyer, but I'm going to feed all the information to Brockman, so he can finally take back the materials. They've never been out of his men's sights."

Zed nodded his head slowly. Something still wasn't sitting right with him, but he couldn't put his finger on it.

"Okay, that takes care of Jefferies," Gray said. "Any sightings of Raymond?"

"Nothing. None of his known aliases have been used at any airport," Dex said.

Marcia's phone rang. Zed saw Lesley's picture come up on the display.

"*Querida*, put it on speaker."

"Lesley, where are you, honey? Are you okay?"

"Marcia," it was clear Lesley was crying. "I can't reach Daddy on the phone. Nobody will tell me anything. Do you know where they are? I need to go see them." She continued to say something, but Zed couldn't understand her through her sobs.

"Lesley, calm down. Are you high?" Marcia's tone was loving, patient, and firm.

"No. No. I promise—"

"Everybody's fine," Marcia cut through Lesley's words. "Tell me where you are, and I'll have someone come and pick you up and take you to the hospital.

Dex already had his phone out, Zed would bet money he was talking to Kane.

"I'm in Alexandria. My friend's name is Margaret, just like Mom."

"I need an address," Marcia stayed on track.

Lesley gave it to her.

"Are you safe where you are?" Marcia asked. "Are you going to relapse being around Margaret and with what's happened?"

The sound of Lesley blowing her nose came across clearly. "I already flushed the shit down the toilet. I just want to get to Daddy and the girls. I'm not going to use this as a crutch."

Marcia slumped against him in relief.

Dex held up five fingers, three times. Marcia straightened and gripped her phone tighter.

"Lesley, someone will be picking you up in less than fifteen minutes."

"Don't hang up," Lesley pleaded.

"I won't hang up until your ride arrives." Marcia picked up the phone and started talking to the girl who meant so much to her.

All the time Marcia had been talking to Lesley, Zed had been listening as Dex had been filling in Harold Brockman about his oldest daughter and the information on Vitoly and Jefferies. Both calls ended at the same time.

Marcia looked up and gave him a weary smile. "Was that Mr. B. on the line?" she asked turning to Dex.

"Yep. He's going to take care of Jefferies now that he knows everything."

"Good job, Dex," Gray said.

Evie reached over on the couch and hugged Marcia. "I'm happy about your sister," she said.

"Lesley's just my friend," Marcia countered.

"She's your sister in every way that matters," Evie disagreed.

CHAPTER FOURTEEN

"I suppose we couldn't very well have lured him to the gun range, huh?" Marcia whispered to Wyatt.

The young SEAL grinned. "We needed to make you look like an easy target," Wyatt whispered back. "Think how shitty I feel that everybody just assumes Raymond will make a move on me?"

They were sitting on the beach, watching Zed and Amelia Jackson swimming in the Pacific Ocean. Somehow Dex had found out Raymond was in California, so the team set up this physical training session for Zed outside of the base, so it would be easier for Raymond to target her.

Despite the fact this was basically a set up, and she was the cheese in the trap, Marcia was enjoying the sun and watching Zed in the water. She had no doubt in her mind, the men of Black Dawn would make sure she stayed healthy.

"You're ogling your man," Wyatt teased.

"You've been having impure thoughts about Amelia, don't lie to me," Marcia grinned at Wyatt.

She watched in fascination as a blush rose up on his face. She'd actually been just kidding him, but apparently, she'd hit the mark.

"Come on, it's about time we went for our little walk." Wyatt helped her up off the sandy beach and they started towards the seagrass. He paused for just a moment, and Marcia realized he must be listening to someone on the communication device embedded in his ear. She'd tried to use one but utterly failed. She always seemed to be talking to thin air, so she told Zed, that for the good of the operation, she wouldn't have one.

"What'd they say?" she asked Wyatt.

"Where Dalton is positioned, he doesn't see anyone. From Griff's vantage point, nothing. They want us to walk up to the bike trail."

They picked their way up the sandy slope, away from the water. As they got closer, a group of runners were coming their way. Wyatt pulled Marcia to a stop.

"Let's let them get by before we go up."

Marcia watched the morning joggers and saw some bicyclists in colorful jerseys coming from the other direction.

Wyatt was pretending to be nonchalant, but she could see that he was listening intently.

"What? What are they saying?"

"Hunter thought he saw something, but it was a false alarm." Wyatt was all business. He kept his hand on her elbow.

"Oh no," she cried and tried to move forward, but Wyatt's grip was implacable. Marcia watched as one of the cyclists careened toward the crowd of runners. The man in the yellow jersey went over his handlebars and took down three runners, his bicycle skidding into two others.

"Report!" Wyatt said.

"They need help," Marcia cried as she saw people sprawled along the trail.

Wyatt turned, so he was between her and the group of athletes. She looked over his shoulder. This couldn't be anything more than an accident.

"I see him!" Wyatt said.

Marcia saw a man over to the right of the accident. She'd thought he was one of the cyclists, but he was hanging back from the mess, removing his backpack.

Wyatt pulled out his gun. A woman screamed. Hunter came out of nowhere and tackled the bicyclist who now had a gun in his hand. The lean SEAL drove the man to the ground. Silence reigned.

* * *

Zed was still wiping down when the commotion started. Amelia had already left to go to her car. This was it, they were finally going to get the bastard.

"Report," he said into his mic.

"Marcia's fine. He was in with the bicyclists. We've got him."

Zed was already on the run to the north, his senses expanding, waiting for—.

"Zed," Amelia cried.

Goddammit, they'd told her she needed to leave the area. What's more, Aiden was supposed to be watching out for her.

Zed turned and saw Raymond had Amelia by the arm.

"Let her go," Zed said. "It's me you want."

"For the moment, it's you. Eventually, it will be your little fuckbuddy." Raymond said as he pushed Amelia forward. He had a gun shoved in her side.

"I'll go with you, just let Amelia go."

"That was quite the nice little set up your team did for me over there." Raymond pointed to the north where a siren could be heard. "Too bad for you, you underestimated me."

Zed looked at Amelia's face. She wasn't doing well. He could see the beginnings of a panic attack. If that happened, Raymond would just kill her and be done with it.

Where was Aiden?

"What pawn were you willing to sacrifice, Felix?" Zed asked Raymond, trying to stall.

"I love the Thorne Group, they always have newbies willing to take side jobs. They make excellent cannon fodder."

Amelia started to tremble, and Zed willed her to keep it together for just a little longer.

"Why not let this go? Jefferies would pay you top dollar to keep you on his team, why not focus on that instead of Marcia?"

Raymond's face contorted in rage. "Jefferies, the Thorne Group, hell, damn near anyone will pay for my services. I'm worth top dollar."

"That's what I'm saying, why screw it all up for revenge?"

"You think this is revenge?" Raymond asked. "This isn't revenge. That little bitch tried to make a fool of me. Nobody is allowed to do that. Especially, not some woman. If you let them get away with that, you're worthless."

"Don't" Amelia's soft voice could barely be heard over the noise of the Pacific Ocean.

"Let her go," Zed pleaded again. Behind Raymond, he saw Aiden pushing himself up off the sand, his head covered in blood.

"You really were a pain in the ass in Borneo," Raymond said flippantly.

Amelia slumped against him, lodging the gun between her and Raymond. Zed jumped. He grabbed Raymond by the head, twisting as Aiden rushed from behind. Zed heard the satisfying crack of Raymond's neck breaking as the gun went off. He turned panicked eyes to Amelia, expecting to see blood seeping up under her wetsuit.

"It looks like you both killed him," Aiden said somewhat groggily.

Amelia was holding the gun. Raymond had been shot in the chest at about the same time Zed had broken his neck.

* * *

"We were supposed to be in this together," Marcia said through gritted teeth. "You didn't tell me you were setting yourself up."

"We weren't sure which way he was going to go," Zed said. "It could have been just as easily you he was after, so you needed to have your head fully in the game. I couldn't have you worried about me." Zed's eyes flashed down at her.

"So, this wasn't about not trusting me?"

"Fuck no. I trust you with my life, Marcia. This is a matter of everyone playing their position. Wyatt's entire focus was on you, he didn't know about our secondary operation, either."

Marcia thought about it and realized Zed was telling the truth. Wyatt had been just as in the dark as she had been, but he hadn't been upset, seemed to think this was a good way of handling things. Maybe she needed to take a page out of his book.

"How's Amelia?" she asked.

Zed started the car and headed toward the apartment.

"Amelia is doing fine, great in fact. Since coming back from Afghanistan, she's been suffering from PTSD and was sure she could never cope with any kind of combat situation again. She said this helped her turn a corner."

Marcia was happy to hear that.

A car tried to merge into them and Zed laid on the horn. He accelerated, so they got out of the dumb butt driver's way, but didn't slow down until they took their exit. It was unlike him.

"Zed?"

He gave her a tight smile. "Almost home."

What the heck was wrong? The bad guy was dead, and Zed seemed to be crawling out of his skin.

As soon as the vehicle was parked, Marcia undid her seatbelt and reached for the door. His big hand landed on hers.

"What do you think you're doing?"

"Getting out of the car?" She gave him a bewildered look.

"You're supposed to wait for me."

"Raymond is dead," she argued reasonably.

"Marcia, did you forget your house in DC was bombed three days ago? We still don't have that figured out yet." Zed's eyes glittered down at her.

"Mr. B. said it had to do with the Saudi's and Yemen," her voice trailed off.

"Until everything is wrapped up to my liking, you follow the safety protocols we've established. Got it?"

She nodded. Zed got out and yanked open her door. Where was her calm, cool, and collected SEAL? Marcia gave him a confused smile as he walked her to the apartment. As soon as they were inside, he slammed the door shut and jerked her into his arms.

Zed's mouth plundered hers, his fingers sinking into hair, while his other hand gripped her ass and pulled her tight against him. For a split-second, Marcia was worried about him, but then all conscious thought dropped away as she spiraled into a pit of need. He maneuvered her against the wall and shoved her tee up and over her head.

Marcia whimpered at their short loss of contact. Before he could ask what was wrong, she twined one arm around his neck, the other hand in search of his heat. She found him, hot and hard, straining against his shorts. She caressed the length of him, needing like she never had before.

Zed worked down her shorts and panties, and when they were partway down her leg, he used his foot to push them the rest of the way to the floor. His fingers found the heart of her, circled and tugged until she thought she would go out of her mind.

"Come for me."

"Not without you," she panted.

He thrust two fingers inside her and everything went up in flames. She couldn't speak, couldn't see, couldn't breathe. When she finally surfaced, she touched the button on his shorts, then suddenly she was upside down.

"What?"

"No condom out here," Zed said as he carried her down the hall to the bedroom. He dropped her onto the bed, and she stared up at him. Where was his wicked smile? Those warm eyes? Instead she was facing a marauder, a man who was intent on conquering. Why?

"What's wrong?"

Zed sheathed himself, then pulled her to the middle of the bed, and pulled her legs over his arms.

"I'll tell you what's wrong," he said as he stroked through her wet folds. "I wasn't with you. When they made their move, it wasn't me there to protect you." Zed slid deep inside her, his eyes never leaving hers.

Marcia felt his possession all the way to her soul.

"It was your team protecting me," she protested.

Zed's hands gripped her tighter, pulling closer, then he rocked forward, so his lips were next to her ear.

"You're mine. It killed me not to be there with you."

She clung to him, peppering kisses along his jaw.

"I was safe because of you," she insisted.

His heart was racing, she could feel it against her breasts. She knew he was barely keeping control, but this man of hers would always keep her safe, and right now she didn't need his control. She dug her fingernails into his back.

"More."

He continued with those same strong, steady strokes that were driving her to the brink of insanity, but she could tell it wasn't what he needed,.

Marcia pulled back and grabbed fistfuls of Zed's hair, glaring at him.

"I'm not made of glass."

"I'll never hurt you," he promised. He was worried.

"Of course not. I know that. But I need all of you." She shoved her hips up, trying to bring him deeper. Trying to show him she was his safe spot.

"Marcia," he begged. "Have a care."

"I need all of you," she whispered the words staring up into his eyes. "Give me all of you."

For a moment she'd thought she'd lost, then he moaned. His lips settled on hers, taking, giving, pleasing, coaxing. He pushed her higher, and she met him, lights skittering across her vision as she reached heights she'd never imagined, up and up until she screamed his name. His real name.

"My Zed. You're mine."

He rolled them over and she sprawled on top of him like she had been through a hurricane.

"I've been yours since the moment I saw your photo," he said solemnly. "We belong to each other."

Marcia needed to understand what he was saying, but Zed started to stroke his hand down her back, and she couldn't stay awake. What photo was he talking about?

* * *

He sat in the chair in the bedroom, watching her sleep. Marcia was beautiful. Had it only been six-and-a-half weeks ago he'd read about her while on the USS Ronald Reagan? Just that short amount of time since he'd first seen her picture?

His gaze flitted over to the picture of his grandmother on the bedroom dresser, and he smiled. He shook his head, thinking back to a time when he hated the idea of having the 'sight' like his abuela. Instead, it had brought him the two most important people to him.

"She's in a better place, Zed," his grandmother said.

She gripped his hand so hard, he almost cried out in pain. Abuelita needed him to be strong for her as they stood at this freshly turned pile of dirt. He was hot, the suit she had bought him for the occasion itchy.

Zed looked up at all of the people who were at the gravesite. Mr. Fuentes from across the street. He was fat. Mrs. Robinson from the seamstress shop. She made really good chocolate chip cookies. Amy, a seamstress who worked for his grandmother. There were more people from the neighborhood.

Nobody said anything about his mom even though it was her funeral. Delores Zaragoza was unknown to most people. They came to support him and his grandmother. Even though he was only in third grade, he understood that.

"Now you throw your flower, Zed," his grandmother told him.

He looked down into the yawning black hole and threw the pretty yellow rose. It made him feel better, maybe it would make Mama happier.

He heard a baby cry. He looked over and saw a woman holding a baby, standing away from the others, staring at Zed. She walked around the grave and came to stand in front of them. Zed strained to look at the toddler's eyes.

"Mr. Fuentes, please take Zed to my car," his grandmother requested.

Zed really wanted to stay and listen, so he bent down and pretended he had to tie his shoe. The lady asked if a man named Carlos had been by after Delores had died.

"Don't speak his name." His grandmother spit on the ground.

The young woman had started to cry, then so did the baby. The baby who was so important to Zed.

"I need to find Carlos," the young woman begged. "Hunter needs food."

Mr. Fuentes grabbed Zed's hand and practically dragged him to Abuelita's car, but not before he saw his grandmother give the girl some money and a kiss on the cheek. She also kissed the top of the baby's head, then made the sign of the cross.

When his grandmother got into the car to take them back to their little house, he asked, "Who were they?"

"Nobody."

He stared intently at his grandmother's sad and tired features.

"Can they come live with us?" Zed asked.

"Don't be silly." He watched as tears leaked down her face.

When they pulled into their tiny little driveway, he saw Mrs. Robinson standing at their door with a plate of cookies in her hand.

"Look, she brought you cookies," he exclaimed, hoping his grandmother would feel better.

"You're such a good boy," she smiled wearily.

Marcia stretched on the bed, and a sharp wind of possessiveness, protectiveness shot through him. She looked over at him, her eyes wide and luminous. Marcia's laughter peeled through the room.

"Yes?" he inquired, raising an eyebrow.

She sat up in the bed and laughed even harder. He felt his own lips twitch.

"You totally lost it. You went into total caveman mode."

He waited.

She crawled off the end of the bed and walked over to him naked as the day she was born.

"Do you know what was even better than that?" she asked softly as she sat down on his lap.

"You loved every minute of it?" he asked drily.

"Well, there is that. But you trusted me." She did a fist pump. "And I trusted myself enough to go cavegirl."

"Yes, you did," he grinned.

They just looked at one another and smiled, realizing they had everything. She kissed the bottom of his jaw.

"So where do we go from here?"

"You can only go back to DC when we know Jefferies doesn't have you in his sights. That's not up for negotiation."

"So, until then?"

"I want to tell you a story."

CHAPTER FIFTEEN

Marcia got out of the shower and headed to the kitchen. It smelled fantastic.

"Dinner and a story, I'm one lucky girl."

"You might not think so at the end. I'm going to be looking for advice," Zed warned as he pulled a beer out of the fridge and went back to slicing bell peppers, zucchinis, and onions. He'd already left a glass of wine for her on the kitchen counter.

"Women love giving advice," Marcia assured him as she took a sip of the Syrah.

She saw him hesitate.

"Zed, just because you ask for advice and I give it, never means I'm going to be upset if you don't take the advice. As a matter of fact, think of it more as if we're talking things over."

She saw his shoulders relax.

"Hunter Diaz is my half-brother, but short of DNA testing, I have no way of proving it." He looked up from his slicing to see how she was taking the news.

"Then how do you know?"

"You. You coming into my life confirmed it."

Marcia was just about to put the wineglass to her lips, when she set it back down and stared at Zed.

"I think I need some of that story time now. I'm totally confused. How do I have anything to do with Hunter being your brother?"

"Marcia, I've trusted many of my gut instincts. I know I'm luckier than most men, and my team puts it down to my intuition which I know I get from *Abuelita*. But it's been nothing like the day I saw your photo in that mission file. This wasn't a matter of me falling in love with a picture, I saw your photo and recognized my soul mate."

Marcia's world stopped. Zed had put down the knife and was looking at her.

"You did?" she queried softly.

"Yes."

Marcia tried to think of some quip she could make, something to lighten the mood. She stared at her man, helplessly. Life with this man just continued to get more amazing. She bowed her head, trying to keep things together, then she looked up at him questioningly.

"I don't understand how this relates to Hunter."

"I always believed Hunter was my brother, but I didn't trust it. I didn't trust in my grandmother's gift until now."

"I know you said you mentored him out of the gang life in East LA, but are you saying it was because you believed him to be your brother?" she asked gently.

"Mentored," Zed laughed derisively. "I used that word, didn't I?"

Marcia nodded.

"Ready for your story?" He threw the vegetables in the frying pan with the steak strips.

"Let me set the table," she said as she grabbed utensils.

Quietly, they got the meal put together, then sat down at the table.

"I'm ready," she said after her third bite.

"Two years after my *abuela* kicked my mom out of the apartment, she died. There was a funeral, and this woman and child showed up. I was only eight, but even I realized she wasn't clean and neither was the baby."

Marcia winced. It must have been bad for a kid to have noticed.

"The woman came up and asked about some man named Carlos I had heard mom and grandma whisper about in the past. That's who this woman was looking for. Before she could say too much in front of me, my grandmother had Mr. Fuentes take me to our car."

Zed stopped eating. "Grandmother gave her money, but it wasn't enough. I asked *Abuelit*a in the car ride home who they were, and she said nobody."

Marcia winced.

"I asked if they could come live with us. She told me no."

"So even at eight years old, you were trying to look out for him."

"Some help I was," Zed's mouth twisted. "Hunter is my best friend, Marcia. I know some of what his life was like with that woman and the man I thought was our dad. I should have forced Abuelita to take him in."

"What do you mean?"

"The name of Hunter's father on his birth certificate is Hector Nuñez."

"So, not Carlos," Marcia said.

"No. But still, what's on a birth certificate doesn't mean anything, my father's name is left blank, and so was the father's name on my mother's birth certificate. That's how we are three generations of Zaragoza."

Marcia couldn't help but smile at the pride in his voice. She would have loved to have met his grandmother.

"So, let me get this straight, you're upset with yourself that, as an eight-year-old kid, you couldn't have protected a child who could or could not be your brother when it was totally out of your control?"

Zed gave a tight nod.

"How did you meet Hunter later to become friends?"

"I heard about a kid named Hunter when I was trying to find a way out of *Las Nuevas Espadas*. Once again, I couldn't help my baby brother, so he was going down the wrong path."

"Stop already, tell me how you *did* manage to help."

Zed tipped back a long sip of beer, then looked at her.

"I took leave when he was fifteen. I found him..." Zed rolled his neck and shoulder. "I did a 'scared-straight' on his ass."

"Huh?"

"I kidnapped him. Just pulled him off Belmont Avenue, stuffed his ass in the back of a van, and took him to a safe-house I'd set up. I spent two days pulling in the big guns, showing him what kind of life he was destined to have—prison, death, or worse."

"What was worse?" Marcia asked.

"Killing an innocent. Second to that was letting down the girl in his life. He just didn't know a way out."

"Until you showed him one," she said softly.

"I told him about the ultimate gang. The SEALs. I told him he could get his shit together now and escape. It wouldn't be easy, but it was possible."

"That's a hell of a story Zaragoza," she smiled. "So, this is how you helped your best friend, huh?"

Zed flushed and nodded.

"Did Hunter ever ask you why you singled him out?"

"I said someone had done the same for me, and I was paying it back."

"And he's never questioned that you two look alike?"

Zed stared at her. "What do you mean?"

Marcia stood up from the table and grabbed his empty plate.

"Men are stupid." She set both of their plates in the kitchen sink. When she turned Zed was behind her.

"I thought it was just my mind playing tricks on me. You think we look alike?"

"Gah!" She pushed at his chest until he backed up, then she marched the couch and plopped down.

"Zed, aren't you and Hunter as close as brothers right now?" she asked, looking at him from under her lashes. She watched him carefully as he stood over her. He was clearly agitated.

"Yes."

"How would you telling him you think or have a voodoo knowing that you're brothers change things?"

He thrust out his chin. "He deserves to know I failed him."

Marcia thought her head might explode.

"When did you fail him?"

"He should have come and lived with me and my grandmother. Marcia, you have no idea how bad it was for him as a little kid before a wonderful woman took him in. It's my fault."

Everything came crashing together. All the answers cascaded through her mind like when she was working on a complicated equation. The misguided sense of guilt he had about not being in two places at the same time on the beach today. It all stems from this. Zed took responsibility for everything, thinking he should have been able to save a two-year-old when Zed himself had only been eight.

"Honey, please sit down, I'm getting a crick in my neck."

"I'm sorry," he said as he sat down and pulled her into his arms.

"So, you wanted my advice, right?"

"Yes," he said warily. God, she could tell he expected her to berate him.

"Here it is. You should absolutely tell him what you think. You should tell him what you remember. Hunter will be overjoyed at the idea of the two of you possibly sharing the same blood."

He sighed.

"But if you expect Hunter to berate you for not fighting for him as a toddler, you're going to be mistaken. This will just be icing on the cake."

"You think?"

"I know."

* * *

"That was really nice of Marcia to invite Aliana down for the weekend. Since Lottie moved, she's been missing her girlfriend time."

The men were seated at the outside bar in a restaurant close to the mall. The ladies were going to be there soon to meet them for lunch. Zed watched as the calamari was put down on their table.

"So, spill," Hunter said. "Are you looking for some advice on how to propose?"

"I think I've got that all covered," Zed's lip quirked, "but thanks."

"Something's up with you. I would have figured after you came back from Virginia, life would be good. Knowing the ambassador in New York was bombed the next day kind of put the whole Jefferies thing to bed."

"No," Zed said. "Knowing the Brockman's being targeted was part of an overall effort and outside of Jefferies made me feel minimally better. I'm not going to feel completely better until Jefferies is dead. At one point, he had his sights on my woman. He might not be a psychopath like Raymond, but still he's out there, and I'm not happy."

"What does Brockman say?" Hunter asked.

"He agreed with Marcia when she called me an over-protective Neanderthal."

Hunter burst out laughing. "That sums you up nicely."

Zed took note of the text that came in on his phone and smiled.

"You agree too?" Zed asked.

"Hell yeah. Not that I don't thank God for it. You saved my ass."

Zed stared at the younger man who was surely his blood.

"No, I didn't, Hunter," he said hoarsely.

Hunter's gaze lasered in on him. "What the fuck do you mean?"

"I should have done more."

"Jesus Christ, I wouldn't be sitting here today, waiting for my woman to come out of Nordstrom's if it wasn't for you. What the hell are you talking about, Zed?"

"I can't be sure because I was only eight, but I'm pretty sure you and your mom came to my mom's funeral."

Zed waited. He watched as Hunter processed the information.

"Are you sure it was me? My mom?"

"No." Zed answered. "Yes."

"Now you're just giving me whiplash," Hunter laughed easily. "Zed, you're about ready to give yourself a heart attack. Just spit out whatever it is."

"I'm pretty damn sure you're my brother. I've thought that for years. I heard my mom talk about a man named Carlos as my father."

"The name on my birth certificate under father is Hector Nuñez," Hunter said slowly.

"I know."

"Zed, if you've checked this out, you know we're not related."

Zed stared Hunter straight in the eye. "We are. You're my brother. I know it now."

"How?"

"These feelings are truer than anything written on a birth certificate. I just know. We can have a DNA test done."

Hunter's black eyes stared at him for long quiet moments. Then he grinned.

"The girls are going to love this."

"You don't understand, I should have done more—"

"Not this shit again. As your baby brother, it's my job to get you to loosen up."

Zed leaned forward on his elbows. "Listen, I'm serious."

Hunter leaned forward too. He stared fiercely into his eyes, "I'm serious too, Zed. In my book, you've always been my big brother. Why do you think you were the first person I called when I needed help with Aliana? If there's blood involved, that just means you can donate a kidney. Not one other thing has changed. I love you."

Zed swallowed. Ah hell, he was going to lose it.

"What'd we miss?" Marcia asked as she dropped a shopping bag into his lap, her eyes surveying Zed's expression, then turning to Hunter.

"I have a brother," Hunter laughed as he pulled Aliana down beside him.

* * *

"The red one," he called out from the bedroom.

"You peeked," Marcia protested. She'd thrown the Nordstrom bag on his lap at the restaurant earlier that evening because she wanted to lighten the mood. She hadn't expected him to look inside. Marcia shimmied into the slim, red sheath dress and walked out of the bathroom. Zed was lying on the bed with his hands behind his head. He looked like a sultan. Actually, he looked like a relaxed and content man, and Marcia couldn't be happier.

"God you're beautiful." She saw his truth shining from his eyes.

The back of her neck prickled, and she turned around. She saw another frame next to the picture of his grandmother.

It contained an old photo of her. She walked over and picked it up. Margaret Brockman had taken it years ago. She turned to Zed.

"Is this it?"

"Yep."

"It's not even a good picture."

Zed was off the bed, putting on his tie.

"The only picture that might take its place is you in a wedding gown."

She stopped fidgeting with the cleavage on her dress and looked up at him.

"Wedding gown?"

She saw his cheekbones flood with color.

"I hadn't meant to say that." He came up to her and cupped her face and looked into her eyes. "Marcia, you know this is where this is heading, right?"

She felt tears prickle. "I'd hoped."

"Well hang onto your hat and expect a proper proposal very soon because we're going to be married before the summer is out."

"What?" she squeaked.

"I just want this perfect for you and with things still unsettled..."

"You only have another two weeks of PT."

"That's one of the things." He grabbed her hand. "Come on, we're going to be late for dinner."

Marcia was swept out the door to his jeep where she waited for Zed to open the car door for her. While Zed was driving to the restaurant, Marcia wiped the palms of her hands on the hem of her dress. Was he going to propose tonight? It would be just like him to mess with her and make her think the proposal was still off in the future.

"Fuck!" Zed yelled out as a Ford F250 pulled out in front of them. He swerved to avoid it.

Crrruunnnch.

Marcia saw stars and smoke as her airbag was deployed when they were hit from behind.

"Zed!" she shouted.

"Marcia, it's going to be okay," he rasped.

She couldn't turn her head. Her car door was yanked open.

"Zed," she shouted again.

"Got her," a man yelled. She was dragged from the jeep. She tried to scream, but she was out of air. Where was Zed?

Oh God, not another van. Her head hit the metal floor.

She heard someone talking on the phone.

"Tell Jefferies we got the target." Marcia whimpered. Oh Lord, her Neanderthal had been right. "We'll be at the marina soon," the driver said.

The van was going a good speed, but she wasn't tied up. She got on her knees to see if she could open the door and jump out.

"Get her!" the driver yelled.

She heard the scuttling as the man in the passenger seat scrambled back to her. He lunged and pulled her away from the door. She toppled back to the floor and she ended up staring up at him. "What do you think you're doing?" he grinned down at her. He smelled foul.

"Leaving," she spat up at him.

"She's a fighter," he yelled up to the driver.

"Leave her alone, she needs to be in good shape when we deliver her to Jefferies."

"I don't have anything to tie you up with, baby. Guess we'll just have to lie here." He rubbed himself suggestively against her. Marcia cringed.

It seemed like hours, and she had had enough. "Get off me."

"You'll try something stupid." He shoved himself lewdly against her again, and Marcia wanted to cry. Where was Zed, he'd promised it was going to be okay.

She started to scream. She couldn't help it, it just was too much.

"Get off her!" the driver yelled.

The sour smelling man rolled off her. "Shut your mouth, or I'll hit you."

Marcia stopped screaming. He was off her that's what she wanted. She felt the vehicle begin to slow down, then finally stop. She started to scream again, hoping to draw someone's attention. Body Odor man slapped his hand over her mouth.

The van door slid open, and two men crawled in. She cowered back. Think Marcia, they want you alive. Driver boy said you needed to be unharmed. It's going to be okay.

"Use this." One of the two men threw a rag at her face.

"What for?" skunk-man asked.

"Gag her. We need to take her to the boat."

If she got out of this alive, she was never going on another boat for the rest of her life, Marcia vowed.

The rag was tied around her mouth, and she was yanked out of the van, then carried like a sack of potatoes toward the sound of water.

"She's pretty, isn't she?" said to the guy next to him. At least he wasn't the one carrying her because then she'd be throwing up behind the rag because of the toxic odor.

"Shut up." The man carrying her went faster, and Marcia saw the stinker falling behind. There were four men taking her towards the boat. She was dizzy because of the airbag, and she was hung over the back of this guy's shoulders, so maybe it was her imagination, but did she just see a shadow pull stink-boy into the bushes?

She looked around, and now she was surrounded by only three men.

Zed! He was coming to rescue her.

It was time to do her part. She twisted, kicked, and bit.

"Bitch, don't make me hurt you."

Another shadow rose from the bushes and pulled down one of the three remaining men. She kicked and twisted more keeping the remaining men's focus on her. Zed would so totally win.

"What the fuck?" the man holding her stopped, his voice high.

"Give her to me." It was Hunter's voice.

She couldn't see anything. "What's going on?" she cried. This was ticking her off.

She felt herself falling as her captor dropped her. The dark ground came hurtling toward her, then she was caught. Somebody pulled off her gag.

"Zed?"

"Nope, I'm Kane." His grin flashed white.

"Where's Zed? Is he okay?"

"Quit flirting and give her to me," Zed rumbled.

"You're alive!" Marcia wriggled out of Kane's arms to throw herself at Zed. "You rescued me."

Dex walked up. "I'd give you a hug, but I don't want my arm chewed off."

"What's going on?" Marcia looked around in confusion.

"We're not quite done. Dex and Hunter are going to pretend to deliver you to Jefferies. I'm going to take the rear," Zed said as he cradled her in his arms.

"I'd go too," Kane said. "But we're worried about Jefferies recognizing SEALs from Virginia."

Marcia gave Zed a pointed look.

"There's no way I'm not going to be there with you," Zed said. "I'll take up the rear."

Marcia nodded reluctantly. She didn't want to do it. She just wanted it to be over.

"How long?" she asked.

"In just five more minutes, *Querida*, you'll be able to call Brockman and it'll be over. But if you need to stop, we'll find another way," he promised.

"No. Let's just get it done."

She saw Kane, Hunter and Dex all share a smile.

Zed gently transferred her to Hunter.

They walked the quarter mile in the dark to the boat.

"Jefferies is expecting us," Hunter said to the man at the top of the gangplank who was holding an automatic rifle. The bald man looked at Marcia and nodded.

Two more guards were on deck, and there was Jefferies, gloating.

"Excellent," he said as he saw Marcia. "Drop her," he pointed to a spot in front of him. Hunter gently lowered her to the wood floor.

"Why do you need me?" Marcia asked. She made her voice quiver.

"Harold was closing in on me. He'll back off to keep you alive."

"He won't give into blackmail, he's too patriotic," she jeered.

Jefferies laughed. "Ever since his wife died, you and his other daughters are his Achilles heel. He'll give me whatever information I want to save you."

She looked at this man who had once been a friend of Mr. B's, and shivered. "You're wrong. If you had one of his daughters, maybe."

Jefferies got down on his haunches and stroked a finger down the bridge of her nose. "Marcia, you underestimate how important you are to Harold."

Jefferies' gaze jerked up, as Marcia heard movement behind her, sickening thuds.

"What?" Jefferies screamed. He yanked Marcia by the hair.

Not a chance in hell, not that again. She kicked, trying to get his junk, his knee, anything. She wasn't going to be a hostage. She thrashed wildly, she didn't want Jefferies to press a gun against her. She didn't!

"Whoa there. Calm down." Zed softly trapped her arms by her sides so she stopped thrashing. It took long moments for Marcia to realize her hair wasn't being pulled anymore, that she didn't have a gun shoved against her. She looked around and saw the three guards, unconscious, and Jefferies on the deck with Dex's foot on his neck. Hunter was on his cell phone.

"How did you find me?"

"Kane and Hunter were following you," Zed said.

"And that's another thing," she said as Kane walked up on the deck. "What's Kane doing in California?"

"Following you," he reiterated.

"Why didn't you tell me?"

"Because you and Harold thought I was out of my caveman mind."

She heard sirens in the distance.

"But Hunter's been in on this all along?"

"He saw me get an incoming text from Kane today while he was trailing you and Aliana. Hunter wanted to help."

"You did the right thing wearing the red," Kane chimed in. Jefferies groaned, and Dex pushed down harder with his foot.

Oops, here it came. Zed was prepared. As soon as the first tear started, he had her in his arms.

"I can't believe how incredibly brave you are."

"I'm not brave," she snuffled against his chest. "I was so scared."

"Me too," he breathed into her hair. "Losing you would end my life. I love you so much Marcia."

"I'm so glad you're a Neanderthal," she whispered. "I couldn't ask for anybody better to keep me safe."

Zed's arms clutched her tight, and she knew she was home.

EPILOGUE

This was the most nervous Zed had been during his relationship with Marcia. He'd thought everything had been fine before he'd left on this last mission. They'd found a townhome in Alexandria, and she was scheduled to start school soon. Hell, it was even back at Virginia State, and when he'd gone wheels up, she'd been spinning around in excitement.

He, on the other hand, was happy to see that life was changing on another front for Marcia. Finally she was not the one always in a support role for the Brockman family. Instead they were more of a source of fun and enjoyment. Especially Lesley. It was like she had her best friend back.

He and Marcia were supposed to be married in just a month. Folding her into his arms last night when he'd gotten home at midnight had been paradise. Her soft limbs, her silky hair and low sighs were the stuff of dreams. But this morning he'd felt her gaze on him before she'd snuck out of bed. She'd never done that before and it had him questioning himself.

Six weeks ago, he'd told her about the man he'd lost on a mission last year. It was one of those midnight moments of sharing, and as soon as the words had been out of his mouth, he worried she would think his job was too dangerous and have second thoughts about marrying him. But she hadn't been like that at all. In typical Marcia fashion, she had surprised the hell out of him by listening and getting him to talk about everything.

She made him really think through how his need to protect everyone might be a little unrealistic. But when he thought about how he'd ultimately ensured her safety against Jefferies, he realized he probably wasn't going to change what he did. He might, however, not think every negative outcome was his fault.

But what was going on with Marcia? She needed to be happy. It was his job to make her happy.

You could just ask, a niggling little voice suggested, but he pushed it away. If she'd wanted to tell him, she would have. Therefore, it was up to him to figure out what was going on and fix it. He got out of bed and stopped short at the guest bathroom in the hallway. The door was closed. What was Marcia doing in there, instead of in the master suite bathroom?

He listened. She was gasping. Was she crying?

"Marcia?" he knocked on the door. He was met by moments of silence, then he heard retching. He pushed the door open to find Marcia kneeling in front of the toilet, vomiting.

"*Madre de Dios.*"

He knelt down naked beside her and caught her as she started to slump to the floor.

"Marcia, let's get you back to bed."

She waved him off, then stuck her head back into the toilet bowl and heaved. Her entire body shuddered like it would rip apart. Zed held her in his arms, making crooning noises, then when she was done, he flushed the toilet. He made sure she was steady enough to hold onto the rim on her own, then he grabbed a washcloth, wet it, and stroked her face, trying to soothe away the sweat and strain.

Marcia gobbled in great gasps of air.

"Do we need to take you to the hospital?"

Her eyes finally seemed to be able to focus, and she stared at him. She was white as a sheet. It reminded Zed of the condition he found her in the jungle all over again. He hauled her up into his arms, strode into their bedroom, and set her down on the bed.

"I'll get dressed. Hospital or urgent care?" he asked. Zed went to his dresser to grab clothes, when Marcia's laughter rang out.

"Neither."

"Should I call Kane? He'll know what to do."

"Zed, you big oaf, this isn't a mission. I'm pregnant. This is morning sickness." The shirt he was holding dropped to the floor.

"Oh Honey, you should see your face."

He came over and cupped hers. "Are you serious?" he rasped.

"Open the closet. There's a gift bag on the top shelf. Go grab it."

Zed continued to stare at her in shock. He'd had no idea. No clue. No feeling. How was this possible?

"Closet," she waved him away. He went to the closet and pulled down a little green gift bag filled with yellow tissue paper. He brought the bag back and handed it to her.

"No, silly, it's for you."

He dug through it and found a small, white plastic wand. When he peered down at the little writing in the window, it said, PREGNANT.

"You're going to be a daddy," she grinned.

"I thought you said this project would take longer," he said. He looked at her resting there in his green t-shirt, looking so delicate.

"You have strong swimmers. We scored in our first month. Apparently, the sicker you are with morning sickness the stronger the pregnancy. I can tell you Zed, it's a strong pregnancy."

Now that he really looked at her, it seemed she'd lost weight she couldn't afford to lose.

"Stop," she held up a hand. "Did I just see Neanderthal Man rear his ugly head?"

He looked back down at the plastic stick, then up at her. "Yes, you did. Deal with it."

"Fudge nugget. You're going to be all overprotective, aren't you?"

"Yes, I am. Overprotective is in the job description."

She crooked a finger at him. He leaned down. "Closer," she whispered.

"Yes?" he whispered back in her ear.

"But you know not every little bad thing that might happen rests on your head, right?" Her deep sherry colored eyes were anxious.

"I've learned my lesson, I know better than that," he assured her.

He pushed his hand underneath her shirt and rested it on her flat tummy.

"But do you want to know something?" he asked her.

Her eyes overly bright, she nodded yes.

"Our little girl is going to be just fine. I just *know* it."

THE END

BIOGRAPHY

Caitlyn O'Leary is an avid reader and considers herself a fan first and an author second. She reads a wide variety of genres but finds herself going back to happily-ever-afters. Getting a chance to write, after years in corporate America, is a dream come true. She hopes her stories provide the kind of entertainment and escape she has found from some of her favorite authors.

As of winter 2018 she has fourteen books in her two best-selling Navy SEAL series; Midnight Delta and Black Dawn. What makes them special is their bond to one another, and the women they come to love.

She also writes a Paranormal series called the Found. It's been called a Military / Sci-Fi / Action-Adventure thrill ride. The characters have special abilities, that make them targets.

The books that launched her career, is a steamy and loving menage series called Fate Harbor. It focuses on a tight knit community in Fate Harbor Washington, who live, love and care for one another.

Her other two series are The Sisters and the Shadow Alliance. You will be seeing more for these series in 2018.

Keep up with Caitlyn O'Leary:

Facebook: tinyurl.com/nuhvey2
Twitter: @CaitlynOLearyNA
Pinterest: tinyurl.com/q36uohc
Goodreads: tinyurl.com/nqy66h7
Website: www.caitlynoleary.com
Email: caitlyn@caitlynoleary.com
Newsletter: http://bit.ly/1WIhRup
Instagram: http://bit.ly/29WaNIh

BOOKS BY CAITLYN O'LEARY

The Found Series
Revealed, Book One
Forsaken, Book Two
Healed, Book Three

Midnight Delta Series
Her Vigilant SEAL, Book One
Her Loyal SEAL, Book Two
Her Adoring SEAL, Book Three
Sealed with a Kiss, A Midnight Delta Novella, Book Four
Her Daring SEAL, Book Five
Her Fierce SEAL, Book Six
A SEAL's Vigilant Heart, Book Seven
Her Dominant SEAL, Book Eight
Her Relentless SEAL, Book Nine
Her Treasured SEAL, Book Ten

Protecting Hope, Book Seven (*Seal of Protection & Midnight Delta Crossover Novel; Susan Stoker KindleWorld*)

Black Dawn Series
Her Steadfast Hero, Book One
Her Devoted Hero, Book Two
Her Passionate Hero, Book Three
Her Wicked Hero, Book Four

Shadow Alliance
Declan, Book One
Cooper's Promise, Companion Novel (*Omega Team and Shadow Alliance Crossover Novel; Desiree Holt KindleWorld*)

The Sisters Series
Tempting Fire, Book One (*Sisters Series and Dallas Fire & Rescue Crossover Novel; Paige Tyler KindleWorld*)

Fate Harbor Series Published by Siren/Bookstrand
Trusting Chance, Book One
Protecting Olivia, Book Two
Claiming Kara, Book Three
Isabella's Submission, Book Four
Cherishing Brianna, Book Five

Made in the USA
Coppell, TX
17 May 2021